BECOMING PRINCESS EDEN

HOW THEY MET

A SEAHORSE ISLAND NOVEL
BOOK ONE

LISA LEE

Becoming Princess

Eden

A SEAHORSE ISLAND NOVEL

BOOK ONE: **HOW THEY MET**

LISA LEE

THE RED PALACE

BUFFER

THE ROYAL HUB

S4 S1 S3
S5 S2
S6
S7
S8

SISTERS OF MERCY

HOSPITAL

CIVILIAN AIRPORT

GOLDEN BOWL PLAZA

FOREIGN QUARTER

Indian Ocean

MERMAN HOTEL

GEYSER PARK

BUSINESS DISTRICT

CULTURAL CENTER LIBRARY

NAVAL DOCK

S16

MILITARY BASE

S14 S15

S13

BUDDHIST CAMPUS

S11 S12

S9 S10

CATHOLIC CHURCH CENTER

THE FARM

ISLAMIC CAMPUS

RESIDENCE HALL FOR GUESTS

RESIDENCE HALL FOR PERMANENT TEMPLE BROTHERS

BOYS' ORPHANAGE

THE TEMPLES CHRISTIAN CHURCH

THE TEMPLES ADMIN OFFICES

CONTENTS

ISBN 978-1-7326290-0-4 (EBOOK)

ISBN 978-1-7326290-4-2 (PAPERBACK)

This is a work of fiction. Names, characters, businesses, places, events, locales, and incidents are either the products of the author's imagination or used in a fictitious manner. Any resemblance to actual persons, living or dead, or actual events is purely coincidental.

Cover Design and Illustration by Patricia Moffett

Editing by Christina Schrunk

Formatting by Patricia Moffett

Printed in the United States of America

Second Edition February 2024

Published by Lisa Lee

Chicago, IL

Lisaleewrites18@gmail.com

www.LisaLeeWrites.com

"Come away, O human child!
To the waters and the wild
With a faery, hand in hand,
For the world's more full of weeping than you can understand."
Excerpted from "The Stolen Child" by W.B. Yeats

"Behold, I send you forth as sheep in the midst of wolves: be ye therefore wise as
serpents, and harmless as doves."
Bible, Matthew 10:16 (KJV)

EDEN, UNPLANNED JOURNEYS

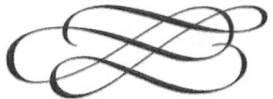

My mother used to say that the only constant in life is change. I would nod like I understood, but I really didn't. I loved my life in Sunny City, New Jersey. Nothing ever changed, but I never wished for change. My father would occasionally teach me history that wasn't approved by Saved America's Bureau of Patriotic Education, but those lessons only made me grateful for the relatively easy life I led. Unfortunately, for me, one sunny day in September, everything changed.

The day started pleasantly enough. My mother and I were baking cookies with my two best friends, Mary and Eliza.

"Eden! Stop eating the cookie dough!" my mother admonished.

"Sorry, it was just a taste to make sure it was sweet enough," I said.

"It's sweet enough," my mom said, but she dropped another spoonful of applesauce into the batter anyway. The price of sugar had gone up again, so we made do with the applesauce we'd made the day before.

I was smiling in anticipation of eating warm, sweet cookies as I mixed the dough, when I heard hard footsteps on the bricked walking path that led to our front door. I was puzzled because the mailman had just left, and the footsteps did not have quite the same even rhythm of my dad's footsteps. One side pressed a little harder on the ground than the other. There was a pause, and then I heard the doorbell ring.

My mother wiped her hands on her apron patterned with bright red cherries and red trim and went to open the door. "Finish mixing and start putting the cookie dough on the sheet. I'll be right back." She inspected herself briefly in the mirror above the key table before opening the door.

"Good Day, Mrs. Edwards. I'm Chief Home Inspector Mark Brown. I've come to do an inspection," a male voice said.

I was immediately filled with a sense of dread.

I was born two years before the Saviors' Revolution, a revolution precipitated and won by a group that saved America from itself. I was taught that in the past, to be an American meant you had certain freedoms. Everyone had the freedom to practice whatever religion they saw fit. Women could live alone and had the right to vote. They could even be unwed mothers. The group called America's Saviors believed those freedoms to be false choices, choices not sanctioned by the one true living God. I never could find the biblical basis for all of Saved America's beliefs, but I knew it wouldn't be a good idea to point this out to anyone.

After the revolution, the new Saved America had hired thousands of inspectors to enforce the new government's home morality rules. Inspector Brown was one of those selected to inspect homes in our small town. He now led a team of Sunny City agents who issued tickets with monetary fines for moral infractions such as an unclean house, unapproved literature, or a rebellious spirit. Not surprisingly, most homes were issued tickets. How else would the inspectors get paid? Still, no one dared protest too loudly. Too many unpaid tickets or major-cause infractions would lead to being branded an untouchable. Never had I been home during an inspection. My parents always arranged for me to be somewhere else when the inspections occurred.

Looking across the kitchen into the living room, I had a good view of our guest. Inspector Brown was a deceptively mild-looking man: medium height, medium build, neutral tan-colored suit and tie, brownish eyes and hair. The brown hair only had a few gray hairs. If a person was given a picture of him and then asked to describe him with their eyes closed, they would be hard-pressed to come up with any distinguishing features. His mild sartorial choices did little to ease my discomfort.

I looked at Mary and Eliza, but they seemed to notice nothing amiss.

"Oh! Please come in." My mother was using her determined bright voice. "Someone was just here about a month or so ago."

"Yes, I like to do random follow-up inspections. I'm sure you have nothing to worry about, Mrs. Edwards." Inspector Brown smiled a most insincere smile as he continued to contaminate our house by walking further into it.

"Oh, how lovely. Cookie baking!" Inspector Brown came to stand behind us girls as we continued putting measured bits of cookie dough onto the waiting baking sheets. He moved a little closer to me and seemed to be looking over my shoulder. I could feel the heat from his body. His cologne was so sharp it felt like someone had taken a stiletto straight through my nose and into my now-aching head.

He moved even closer, surprising me. I dropped my spoonful of cookie dough on the table instead of the baking sheet. Mary and Eliza looked at us, their spoons paused midair.

"Shall I show you the house, or do you want to tour without me in your way?" my mother interjected. I had never heard her voice so bright and brittle.

"You know, I don't think I need to see anything else today," Inspector Brown said as he ran a finger down my arm. "Perhaps you should dress your daughter more modestly, Mrs. Edwards. It is one of the more important virtues. Don't you agree?"

I was wearing a pale-blue short-sleeved summer dress fastened with red heart-shaped buttons down the front and finished with red scalloped trim around the neck and hemlines. I was thirteen and starting to fill out, so the dress was slightly snug across my chest and hips. It was warm in the kitchen, so I'd taken off the cardigan I had worn earlier.

The inspector's words made me feel ashamed and smeared. Inside my heart, I could also feel anger gathering like clouds before a storm.

My anger scared me, and I focused my eyes straight down to the table and prayed silently in my head for him to leave.

"Yes, of course," my mother replied. She told me to go and change as she walked Inspector Brown to the door. Apparently, he only had time to inspect me and not the house.

As I went upstairs to change, I noticed my mom did not ask if he wanted tea or coffee. She usually offered guests something, wanting them to feel welcome in our home. Maybe that was just the case for invited guests. When I came back downstairs, dressed in a loose-fitting brown dress and sweater, Inspector Brown had left.

My mother looked at me and said, "I have a headache. I'm going to lie down."

Surprised, I looked after her with my mouth hanging open.

"Is your mom ok?" Eliza asked, her warm gray eyes filled with concern.

"I guess," I replied, wondering if I should go up and check on her.

"We're not supposed to be unsupervised," Mary said primly as she finished putting the last spoonful of cookie dough on her baking sheet.

I winced a little. I liked Mary as a friend, but sometimes I felt that she liked rules more than she liked people.

"What do you want us to do? Call our mommies and daddies and tattle on Mrs. Edwards?" Eliza asked sharply. "Besides, is that really the most important thing right now?"

I didn't want to talk about Inspector Brown. "Let's just finish baking so you'll have cookies to take home," I said. I wanted to say words that would put my friends and me at ease with each other again, but worrying about my mother and Inspector Brown prevented me from formulating the right ones. In the end, we sat silently as the cookies baked, Mary and Eliza exchanging wordless glances. Despite the delicious aroma of baking cookies, the happy contentment of the fall afternoon had all but disappeared from our sunny kitchen.

After Eliza and Mary left with their brothers who came to walk them home, I started to clean up and put the remaining cookies away. My mother came down when I was almost finished.

I wanted to ask her about Inspector Brown's visit, but she was wiping down the already clean kitchen table and chairs quite briskly. The table was long and thick, made of repurposed cedar wood, and could withstand her vigorous scrubbing. When she got to the chairs, however, I feared the chairs might splinter from the force with which they were being rammed back into their proper place.

My mother could be quite cutting when she was angry, so after the cookies were put away, I busied myself with watering the pots of thyme, mint, and rosemary hanging next to the window by the kitchen sink. Then I heard a strangled sob and turned around sharply.

My mother was crying, her head in her hands and her shoulders heaving. I was at a loss and more than dismayed. I was still a child and didn't want my mother to prove fallible.

I went over and hugged her from behind, my cheek resting on her back. She sighed, and some of the tension eased out of her. But when she turned to face me, her eyes were sad and her demeanor a little wilted.

"Honey," she said. "Let's go for a walk."

So, we walked. We walked down our block and over walking paths of the Sunny City Gardens. Normally, I loved the gardens. They were meticulously groomed, like old English gardens, with row after row of tamed greenery that was somehow serenity-inducing. There was nothing I liked better than to find a quiet space in the gardens to be alone with my thoughts. Of course, I was never truly alone for I always had a chaperone—usually my mother—and there were always other serenity seekers in the park as well. It was more like companionable solitude.

Today, though, the beautiful gardens with their lovely floral scents and flitting birds and buzzing bees only served to highlight my inner anxiety. I was almost angry that the usual pleasure I found in the gardens had been stolen from me by Inspector Brown.

As I walked with my mother, I waited for her to say something that would make everything all right, that would explain Inspector Brown. My waiting was in vain. My mother led us to a sturdy bench under a thick tree with a huge canopy. Both of us sat. I rested my head on her shoulder, and she put her arm around my shoulders.

"Your father and I have decided you should go away to school," she said.

I jerked my head up and looked at her like she had two heads. I had always been homeschooled by my mom. She didn't even let me do Sunday school without her until I was eight. Now, five years later, she wanted to send me away to school?

"I don't want to go away to school," I replied, more confused than defiant.

"I don't want you to go either, but I think—we think it would be best for you. We considered sending you last year, but we agreed to send you for the fall term coming up. You are almost old enough to be married," she replied.

"No one gets married until they are at least sixteen, and that's only if they have to," I retorted.

"The legal age of marriage is fourteen with parental consent," she said. "You are too young to understand how deeply a man's soul can be corrupted by evil. Trust me when I say that if Inspector Brown wanted to marry you, he could, regardless of your age. Most likely, he will . . . he'll . . ." she stuttered. She took a breath and plunged ahead. "He'll treat you as his wife without actually marrying you and accuse you of the sin of enticing him."

"But that would make me a . . ." I said, stunned.

"Exactly," my mother replied.

"How will going away to school stop him?" I asked.

My mother's eyes slid away from mine. "Because the school we've chosen doesn't allow men in at all. Not even to work at the school. They have good security."

"But what about when I come home?" I asked, wondering if all my family vacations would be spent looking over my shoulder for Inspector Brown.

"No, I will come to visit you, and we could meet up with your father off campus." But she still wasn't looking at me when she said it. "Do you remember Ruth and Ruby?"

I nodded. They were girls from the neighborhood who were a couple of years older than me, so while I had spoken to them in passing,

I hadn't had any prolonged conversations with either of them. They were brown girls like me, born before the revolution and adopted afterward. I hadn't seen them or their parents for a while. "Did they move?"

My mother replied, "No one here has seen them recently. They were taken in the middle of the night, and the last anyone heard, they were in Untouchable City."

I gasped in shock. I had never actually been to Untouchable City, but I had heard the name whispered about in such horrified tones that I imagined the city as some kind of dirty gray hell, filled with despairing, unrepentant sinners.

"For what? They seemed like nice girls."

My mother just shook her head. "They didn't just seem like nice girls. They *were* nice girls. Their only crime was that they couldn't fight Inspector Brown." I noticed that my mother lowered her voice and looked around cautiously when she said Inspector Brown's name. "Their parents didn't have a lot of money."

"Well, we're not poor," I said.

"But we're not rich," my mom replied. "Fortunately, your Aunt Adeline has agreed to pay for your schooling. Isn't that a blessing?"

"Yes," I answered automatically, still stuck on the fact that my parents wanted to send me to school.

"Speaking of blessed," my mother said, her real smile returning a little. "Give me your purse so I can put your pocket money in it."

Before I could pout and say I could put money in my own purse, my mom handed me back my purse and was standing up, signaling an end to our conversation. I sullenly followed as she walked, resenting being treated like a three-year-old and confused about the whole conversation.

I expected my transition to school to be as well-managed as all other aspects of my life. A master to-do list would be written. Clothes selected, washed, ironed, mended as needed, and neatly folded. A third-hand set of tan and light-beige luggage pulled out from the closet. A church "send-off" where all the members of the church said a prayer for my safety and well-being.

I loved our church, even though I had to admit that I loved the socializing and potlucks as much as, if not more than, the sermons. Since sugar had been ridiculously expensive the past few years due to a sugar cane disease, special church events were normally the only times I was privileged to enjoy treats made with real sugar.

So, I was surprised when my mom walked us to a very expensive dessert and ice cream parlor and told me to order what I wanted. Unfortunately, devouring spoonful after spoonful of chocolate ice cream distracted me from noticing the oddity of the situation. My mother never splurged, not ever. But today she sat with a funny little smile on her face and asked me if I wanted another cup of ice cream. As I debated whether it would be too gluttonous to say yes, in walked my Aunt Adeline.

"Eden! Clarissa! So lovely to see you both!" We rose from the table and exchanged hugs and air kisses—an affectation of my aunt's.

"What are you doing here?" my mother asked.

"Just came to get—Oh! I forgot my wallet in my car. I'll just get it and come back. Eden—you want to walk with me?"

I looked at my mother, who nodded yes. I grabbed my blue-jean purse out of habit—my mother always lectured me if I left my purse— and followed my aunt. Out in the parking lot, Aunt Adeline had parked her small two-seater between two big vans that weren't exactly minding the lines.

"I hope they don't hit your car getting out," I said.

"I hope not either. Eden—can you go to the right and reach in and get my wallet? My hips won't fit through as gracefully as yours will."

I rolled my eyes and moved as my aunt had instructed. Before I could react, the side door on the van behind me opened and large rough hands grabbed me about the waist and mouth and pulled me into the van. I heard my aunt gasp, but then the van door slammed shut.

My captor's body lurched sideways, and I did too as the van started moving. In a panic, I struggled. My hands pushed with useless effort against massively tattooed and ripped arms, and I strove to drive my feet against my captor's kneecaps. It was like being held by a granite giant. I switched tactics and raised my arms to scratch his face.

He turned me around fast and backhanded me, knocking me back against a passenger seat. He put a heavy knee across my thighs and handcuffed my hands to a steel bar hanging from the inside of the car roof.

I tried to rise, but he backhanded me again, harder this time. Again, I fell back, my tears of pain mingling with blood from my split lip. I opened my mouth to cry out, but he raised his hand again, smiling a smile that was not a smile, and raised an eyebrow in inquiry. I closed my mouth.

He fastened a seat belt around me with one hand while locking my ankles together with another set of handcuffs. I immediately felt ashamed that I hadn't tried to cry out. I thought to myself that I should scream, but it was like fear had sucked the air from my lungs and all rational thought from my mind.

The menace sat his huge hulking presence directly across from me, his swarthy face shaded by a black baseball cap.

"Please, let me go," I managed to whisper.

The menace slowly shook his head, his eyes like blue orbs of ice.

I looked down and saw the wet stain across my lap and realized I had peed on myself. I began to cry in frustration and futility. Thirty minutes ago, I had a happy life. In thirty minutes, my spirit had been broken.

I couldn't think ahead because I was afraid of what came next. So, I tried to stop thinking, to put my brain in an inert state, but the stress of not thinking gave me a headache. My head began to ache, along with my suspended arms and swollen jaw. I could feel the tears, blood, and snot that had started to gel on my cheeks and chin.

It was hard to judge time. The windows were darkened, and the car moved without stopping much. I realized I couldn't hear outside traffic at all, so perhaps it wouldn't have made a difference if I'd screamed before. I closed my eyes and prayed silently for help.

Eventually, I started imagining myself getting rescued. The car would come to a sudden stop, and we'd be surrounded by cops. The menace and driver would try to escape but would be gunned down or caught, and my parents would run to hold me. I must have fantasized myself into dreamland because I awoke with a jerk as the car really did come to a sharp stop. There was a knock on the van door, which the menace immediately opened.

"About time you boys got here," said the woman standing at the door. "It's time for my sherry and bed." The woman who spoke was stout, with a round face topped off with a pug nose, narrow blue eyes, and thin, uncompromising bloodless lips pinched together in a straight line. She was medium height but broad, making for quite an imposing figure. Her eyes looked me up and down and showed no pleasure in my appearance. I fought the urge to shrink back.

"Please," I croaked out. "You have the wrong girl. My parents will—"

The woman interrupted with a guttural laugh followed by a snort. "Your parents are the ones who sent you here."

2

GIDEON, MY BROTHER'S KEEPER

On the other side of the world, exactly thirteen hours ahead, lay the island known as Seahorse. In the shape of its namesake, the island was home to the world's most exotic plants and flowers. Purple grasses and magenta flowers bloomed voraciously. Small imported trees dotted the landscape, especially near the communal homes. The air over the island was frequently hotter than the air over the water surrounding it. The subsequent fog draped the island, hiding then revealing then hiding again.

Never completely hidden was the mountain range at the northern end of the island. The tallest peak stood tall and impervious between her shorter sisters. This statuesque mountain could be forgiven her vanity, as she was adorned with a quite extravagant royal palace. The palace was simply called The Red Palace for the color of the mountain rock from which it was carved. Strategically placed lights gave the palace a soft glow that radiated gently at night over the northern edge of the island. Under a full moon, the island looked surreal, a dream longed for or imagined. Now, though, a blazing hot sun signaled the arrival of a new day. It was not just any day either. Today was the day of the Supreme Fighter Championship.

Twenty-two-year-old Prince Gideon Li, one of the competitors, shadowboxed as he checked his muscular form in the mirror. He was warming up in his palace suite. After a few minutes, he saw Luke, one of the royal guards, behind him in the mirror. Annoyed, he asked, "What is it?"

"Your grandmother is on her way," the guard replied.

"Ugh." Gideon stopped boxing and began running in place as he looked at the screen above the mirror. "Screen, find grandmother."

He groaned when he saw his grandmother's image appear on the screen. She was carrying a tea set. At the slow, tortuous pace she was going, it would take her a while to reach his suite. The tea set meant she wanted to chat. She probably meant to wish him well, but he didn't want to be late to the fight.

"You won't be late," Luke said, as though he read his mind. "She'll be here in about fifteen. If you can keep the conversation to no more than another fifteen minutes, we'll have time."

Gideon nodded as he went back to shadowboxing. Luke left the room, and Gideon found himself thinking about his grandmother as he went through routine moves. She had come to the island as a child refugee, part of the last wave of refugees permitted on the island. More times than he cared to remember, especially when she was by a window, his grandmother would talk with him about how she expected to see the shanties that were there when she arrived and how it always gave her a little jolt to see the island's development. Now there were large communal homes, well-ordered streets, luxury boutique stores, and business districts. And even though she had lived in The Red Palace almost all her adult life, his grandmother had never adjusted to the palace's vastness and formality.

Glancing at the screen above the mirror, Gideon observed her rebellion against the modern changes. Staff rushed to take the tea tray from her hands, but she just shook her head at them. She could have asked her personal maid to have the kitchen staff make the tea and then have a royal page deliver it to Gideon. But that would not do for his grandmother. She'd most likely heated the water on a little hot plate she had added to the small kitchen in her suite and made a simple green tea for him.

It was a long way to Gideon's suite from his grandmother's. Sixty years ago, she would have covered the distance in no time, but now he knew her knees probably creaked and her shoulders most likely ached just from the carrying the tea tray. She was winded and looked a little bit cross as she arrived at his suite. Gideon couldn't imagine why she'd brought the tea all the way to his room.

"Ya Ya, what are you doing here?" Gideon asked as he bent down to take the tea tray. His grandmother's real name was Priya, and she hated to be called Granny. Somehow Gideon and his twin had ended up calling her Ya Ya.

"If you bothered to visit me, I wouldn't have to make the long trek down to your room," she replied irritably as she sat down with a huff.

"Ya Ya, I see you at dinner practically every night," Gideon replied, still standing as he wondered what was going on.

"I had a disturbing dream again last night. I had to warn you," Priya said.

Gideon groaned. "Ya Ya, the fight is today. I must get ready. Tonight, tell me your dream, ok?" He put the tea tray on a side table and extended a hand to help her up.

She turned her head and remained seated. "The dream was worse this time."

"Ya Ya, do you ever have a good dream?" Gideon asked. "Why don't you dream about something nice, like finding a gold mine or the love of my life or something like that?" He held his hand out again.

She slowly stood with his help, but instead of letting go of his hand, she held on and gripped his forearm with her other hand, digging in with her nails. She stared into his face.

"I dreamed of the snake again, but this time you were sitting at a table, looking with horror as blood dripped from your fingers while the snake slithered with glee toward you. I fear evil has already been set in motion. You must be careful. Promise me!" she pleaded.

Gideon nodded, shrugging off her words. He was a man who prided himself on being ruled by reason, so to acknowledge that he always feared her dreams would be a step too far for him. If her dreams frequently came true, it was just a coincidence, he rationalized.

"Did you warn Gabe too?" he asked, always curious as to whether she had come to him first or to his twin Gabriel.

She shook her head. "I only saw you in the dream."

"So, you only brought me tea?" he asked.

Priya sighed, clearly irritated he wasn't more serious about her warning.

She stepped close to Gideon and stretched her arms up to hold his face in her hands before replying, "Yes, I only brought you tea. You are my most favorite grandson."

Gideon smiled at her and was glad that she smiled back, but then she returned to the business at hand.

"Because you are my most favorite, my heart would break if something happened to you. I know you think I am just a crazy old lady—"

"No, Ya Ya . . ." Gideon interrupted to deny, even though it was true.

She slapped his cheeks gently. "Listen to your elders. You must be careful. Don't get caught up in stuff you shouldn't be involved in. Ok?"

"Ok," he replied before giving her a quick hug and walking her to the door of his suite. "I have a fight to get ready for. Wish me luck!"

As he rushed to get ready to leave for the fight, he noticed the small black-and-white photograph of his grandparents on the same side table where he had placed the tea set. He couldn't help but think about their past. Even if he hadn't been in a rush, Gideon would have had little desire to learn more about his grandparents' history than what he already knew. It wasn't so much that he didn't care as much as he didn't find their histories relatable.

He knew his Ya Ya was only seven when she first arrived on Seahorse Island in 2062 with her grandmother, mother, and stepbrothers. In those days, the island had become a haven for those refugees displaced by the submersion. The submersion happened when a massive storm submerged the entire country of Bangladesh, parts of India, Nepal, Bhutan, Myanmar, and a very thin sliver of China. Countries less affected by the submersion had agreed to take in refugees, but only those who met their stringent entry criteria. Unwanted refugees had no place to go and floated from country to country, seeking entry and finding none. Those who lived survived on donated food that had expired and was basically unmarketable. It was an unsustainable situation that was resolved by the appearance of the island, which emerged after the submersion, a miraculous occurrence that baffled scientists.

Eventually, those unwanted refugees found a home on the island. The UN soldiers patrolling the island tried to catch the refugees but never knew where to send them once they caught them, so the refugees stayed. The abundant sea life in the waters surrounding the island nourished their rail-thin bodies, and the island soon became filled with makeshift shanties. The refugees reveled in their new home while making friends, meeting neighbors, and having babies. The island, however, had no real leader or system of government, and crime ran rampant. Also, an unfortunate number of refugees fell prey to diseases caused by the island's unsanitary conditions.

Two years before Priya and her family's arrival to the island, her future husband, Steve Li, stepped into this power vacuum. Li was credited with the island's prominence and affluence of the current day. Gideon had learned an extremely sanitized version of his grandfather's life from history books, but his Ya Ya was not reticent about explaining the complete, unvarnished truth about Seahorse Island's first king, including those parts she didn't really know but had heard about.

The story Priya had been told started prior to Li's coming to the island. He was raised in rural China at a center for children left behind by parents who lived and worked in China's cities. At ten, tired of waiting for his parents to claim him, Li ran away to Guangzhou and was promptly recruited into a local gang specializing in robbing and repurposing electronic toys like phones, watches, and notepads. Li spent his tween years doing on-the-job training for how to steal, strip, and resell electronic devices for those who didn't want their every move monitored by the government. Like most street boys, he was forced to fight frequently in encounters with rival gang members.

At twenty, Li was a man of medium height, with a lean but muscular build, hard face, penetrating gaze, and an uncanny understanding of human psychology. He decided he wanted to be his own boss. He trained in martial arts, read management and pop psychology books, monitored politics, and observed people. At twenty-three, he moved to

Hong Kong. By twenty-five, he had taken over his own gang specializing in illegal tampering with electronic equipment and systems. His criminal empire, however, was hampered both by more powerful gangs and the effectiveness of Hong Kong's Internet Crimes Division. Seahorse Island sounded like a good place to run his business with no interference.

"What do you think happened after your grandfather got to the island?" Gideon's grandmother asked him one day when he was nine. It was the day after the New Year's celebration. Gideon and Gabriel were in the playroom that connected their rooms. They had just started playing a video game, which they were only allowed to play on school holidays and, even then, on a limited basis.

"What?" Gideon mumbled in reply. Gabe was too absorbed in the game to even hear their grandmother.

"Stop your game!" Priya said shrilly. The boys looked at each other in dismay before looking up at their grandmother who had stopped in the doorway. Still, their fingers lingered hopefully near the games' controls.

"You two did a report on the history of Seahorse, right?" she asked.

"Ya Ya, we turned in our reports last week," Gideon explained, hoping that would appease her.

"Really? I was here practically from the time the island started, and you didn't ask me anything," Priya said as she entered the room and sat down on a nearby chair.

The boys looked at each other again. They knew that tone in their grandmother's voice meant they were in for some sort of lecture. But they only had an hour to play before they had to get ready for bed.

"Ya Ya, you always say you hated those days," Gabe replied, bewildered.

His grandmother just shook her head and said, "Still, you should have asked."

"Do you want to talk about it now?" Gideon reluctantly asked.

"No, I hated those days," Priya said.

"What was so bad about those days?" Gabe asked. "Uncle Michael always says you've lived a life of leisure since you married our grandfather."

"You think it's great eating fancy foods as you look out the window and see refugees being turned away, probably to their deaths? Your grandfather wouldn't even let anyone hand out bags of food." Priya became more agitated as she spoke.

"Is that why you insist on the family donating to food charities every year?" Gideon asked.

"Yes," she replied as she got up to leave. She paused at the door. "Don't ever be a leader who eats comfortably in front of beggars."

The boys nodded and breathed a sigh of relief as she finally left their room. They resumed avidly playing their video game.

Afterward, Gideon lay awake longer than usual, puzzled by his grandmother's words and her dislike of the island's early days. From all accounts, his grandfather was a savior. He realized early on that the island needed what he had taken for granted in Hong Kong: a functioning government, a steady and reliable food chain to supplement the fish, some sort of sanitary system, and an electric grid.

Through his grandfather's ingenious negotiating skills, his organization became the first point of contact for those who wanted to know more about the island. He controlled aid that was delivered, and his word was the law. Still, Gideon's grandfather realized the island was woefully underprepared for any challenge to the island's autonomy, so he set out to make friends.

In the end, through diplomacy that rivaled any seen by a first-world country, Seahorse Island became known as Geneva East, a neutral place for the world's leaders to relax, meet, and play. Every amenity was accommodated. Gideon's nine-year-old self was always confused as to why people referred to amenities in hushed tones. He did understand, though, that it was at this point that the island was divided into sixteen sectors. Each sector's development was financially sponsored by a first-world country. In exchange for such largesse, the sponsoring country got a share of the profits produced by that sector for the following ten years and accommodations without charge for their current leader for the following fifty years.

For some reason, the fine print in this deal went unreported. Once each sector completed its ten years of profit sharing, the island would become a sovereign country. So, two generations later, Seahorse was a sophisticated, first-world island with its own military and police force. Its laws forbade some of its prior activities like human trafficking and other morally unacceptable activities.

Instead, the island had arable land, clean water, and reliable electricity. One of its main crops was its unique plants that were discovered to have cancer-fighting properties. These plants did not adapt well to the climate of other countries. Seahorse Island had luck, beauty, and money. What it did not have was a democracy.

In the summer of 2072, the representatives of the sixteen sectors declared Steve Li as King of Seahorse Island and established the rules for the permanent monarchy. The flag was immediately modified from sixteen white doves flying toward an unseen destination to sixteen white doves flying around a yellow circle representing the sun that was the king. The flag's background remained sky-blue to represent the sea and sky.

According to the story Priya often told Gideon, the king saw her one day and ordered her to marry him. But the day after Priya interrupted his video game playing with Gabe, Gideon was playing the Royal Game of Ur with his great-uncles, who told him a much fuller story.

Priya's stepbrothers were the architects of The Red Palace. They were selected soon after Steve Li became king. One day in 2074, the forty-four-year-old king went to see the construction progress on the palace and saw nineteen-year-old Priya for the first time.

According to the elder great-uncle, Joseph, "In those days, Priya was very beautiful, a gorgeous young lady. And she would frequently bring homemade lunches for us." Then Joseph dabbed at his eye with a monogrammed handkerchief.

The younger great-uncle, Michael, disagreed. "Beautiful? She's not the hag she is now, but beautiful is stretching it." He sat back with his hands over his well-fed stomach, satisfied with his pronouncement.

"Anyway," Joseph continued, annoyed that his flow had been interrupted. "As I was saying, Priya would frequently bring our lunches. This allowed her to speak briefly with one of the junior architects, Adam. Everyone knew they liked each other and assumed marriage negotiations between our respective families would start soon. But the king was quite taken with Priya's beauty and assumed all sorts of lovely things about her based on her face alone."

Michael interrupted, "And you know what they say about assuming things."

"No, I don't know what they say about assuming things," said a female voice from the doorway. It was Priya. She gave her stepbrothers a baleful look before stalking off.

"I told you she has the sight," Joseph whispered.

"Yeah, there's something wrong with that woman, all right. All the women in our family are crazy, always seeing things and whatnot," Michael complained.

"Well," Joseph began, "there is a long history of female shamans in our family, but it didn't really take special sight for Priya to realize she couldn't turn the king down. Not without consequences for us, her family."

"Oh, there you go again, yakking on about what a great sacrifice she made for us. We wouldn't have eaten our New Year's dinner in this palace if not for that wedding. She turned up roses, that girl," Michael said smugly.

"True," Joseph conceded. "But she never loved him."

"She didn't?" Gideon asked.

The brothers looked at him as though they had forgotten his presence. Joseph recovered first. "Not as much as she loves you."

Gideon smiled, but he had one more question. "But what happened to Adam?"

"He went on a mission overseas, last I heard," Michael said, and Joseph nodded.

Years later, Gideon was no longer a child easily appeased, but a man fully grown. On that day, he and his twin brother would fight, along with representatives from all sixteen sectors, to hold the title of Supreme Fighter, an ostentatious title that carried a small financial award but larger bragging rights. Unlike his grandfather, Gideon had more charm than violent tendencies, but he still wanted to win that title.

Prince Gideon Li loved the crowd. Even better, the crowd loved him back. Once his name was announced, he put on a mini show of kicks and jabs and flying-tiger moves, to the roaring approval of the crowd. He was ready to fight his third match in two hours. He was confident that he would win this match too, even though it was against his twin brother, Gabe.

He strutted across the mat and roared as he raised his fist to the crowd. He was rewarded with thunderous foot stomping, clapping, and shouts of support. Gideon's parents, however, kept their usual stoic expressions and clapped sedately.

Gideon thought how he would love to rub a victory in his brother's face. Gabe usually won most of their matches in practice, but in the last few weeks, Gideon had won about half the matches with his brother.

After Gideon left the mat, his brother performed similar moves. If the applause and foot stomping were a little louder, Gideon figured it was just due to his brother being older by a few minutes and the heir to the throne. Seahorse Island's subjects were experts at the art of sucking up.

Shrugging off the thought, Gideon spit excess saliva into a nearby cup, moved to the mat, and assumed a fighting stance. He ignored the unusually humid day, the copious amounts of sweat pouring down his back, the slight stench even in the outdoor arena, and the shouts and screams of the crowd. His only thought was to crush his brother to the mat for a decisive victory.

His brother seemed to be in top fighting form. Each time Gideon attacked, his brother expertly blocked him. Gideon had been a fighter long enough to not get frustrated. If he did, his emotions would rule, and he would inadvertently let his guard drop.

His patience was rewarded when his brother didn't move fast enough to block one of Gideon's offensive moves. Unfortunately, as his brother went down, Gideon let his concentration slip a little and was caught off guard when Gabe swung his foot and knocked Gideon off his own feet.

Gideon rolled and moved to get back up, but his brother heaved himself on top of Gideon and whispered, "Please stay down."

There was no way Gideon was going to listen to that plea. He elbowed his brother and flipped so that he was the one holding Gabe down. What he saw shocked him. Gabe's face was grayish blue.

Thinking quickly, Gideon rolled off and clutched his leg while grimacing in feigned pain.

His brother stood up, swaying a little, and on the count of ten, Gabe was declared the winner of the Supreme Fighter title.

In the screaming and shouting that followed, not many people noticed that the towel given to Prince Gabriel hid an inhaler or that when he finally raised his arms in victory, his trainer kept his arm around the prince's waist in support, not in celebration.

Gideon got to his feet and remembered to limp as he walked over and stood next to his brother on the opposite side of the trainer, applauding. When he saw his brother slightly lean his way, Gideon put his arm around him and smiled.

The king and queen's stoic expressions didn't change. They sat in the section of the arena reserved for the royal family, behind glass designed to repel weapons. Not surprisingly, this section was heavily secured with the elite Royal Guard.

As the king stood, everyone else promptly stood as well, and the king's image immediately became visible on every large screen in the arena. The celebratory noises became silent. Reverence for the king was a key patriotic duty.

The king said, "Citizens of Seahorse, in celebration of Prince Gabriel's victory today, a public celebration will be held tomorrow night at the Golden Bowl Plaza. The event will be hosted by the royal family."

Prolonged applause and wide grins greeted this news. A good fight followed by free food and wine was indeed a cause for celebration. The only citizens unhappy with the day's turn of events were the unlucky gamblers who had bet on Prince Gideon.

The king turned toward the fighting area. His sons and the other sixteen fighters bowed deep in a display of unified respect. The king and queen left first, accompanied by various ministers and guards. Then the other royals left, accompanied by their own staff. Celebratory music played as the fighters left to go back to their respective communal homes. The princes returned to the limousine that would take them to their own home, The Red Palace.

Gideon wanted to speak with his brother as soon as they were in the limousine. Unfortunately, the princes were accompanied by their personal guards, Luke and James. Their personal guards had been personally selected by the king. Any misstep by the princes, no matter how minor, was reported to the king. Thus, the princes were prompted to, at least privately, nickname the guards Royal Snitches 1 and 2. The brothers had agreed early on to have personal conversations without those two present. So, Gideon resolved to keep his questions to himself for a little while longer.

Gabe sat across from him, his head back and his eyes closed. He looked as though blood flowed through his veins again, but his extreme tiredness was almost palpable to Gideon. He and Gabe called it their "twin sense." They could each feel when the other was in distress. This bond was made clear when the twins were six-year-olds. In truth, Gideon only half-remembered his hospital stay that year, but his mother loved to retell the story so much that Gideon could tell it himself almost verbatim.

One summer day when he and his brother were six, their mother, Queen Jasmine, hosted a summer solstice party. Her sisters and some of her cousins were visiting, and she wanted to celebrate. The party was outdoors, with the abundant scents from the large potted flowers mixing with that of grilled meat, sweet pastries, savory pastas, exotic sauces, and other favorites of the queen and her guests. Most of the guests were family, so the atmosphere was relaxed with the adults talking, laughing, and perhaps drinking a bit more than they should.

The kids, sensing their parents were not really paying attention, ran rampant like packs of wild animals. The parents didn't worry, assuming their various nannies were looking after the kids. Unfortunately, the mostly middle-aged nannies could not completely keep up with the organic honey-fueled energy of their charges. Between the laughter, conversation, eating, drinking, and the constant roving of the kids, no one noticed little Prince Gideon make his way all alone back into the palace.

When the prince had been gone about five minutes, his twin brother, Prince Gabriel, stopped abruptly in the middle of playing and shouted, "Gide!"

The other kids paused in their play, unsure whether this was part of their game or not. The nannies looked around in panic, realizing they were short one kid.

"Gide!" Gabe shouted again before running to his mother, the queen.

"Gide's hurt," he said as he reached his mother.

The queen looked first for Gideon and then his nanny. She saw neither. The nanny had run inside to look for Gideon.

"Let's go look inside," she suggested to Gabe, assuming Gideon had gone inside to use the washroom or play inside away from the crowd. Sometimes too much noise caused him to retreat to a quiet area.

"Hurry, Mother! He's hurt!" Gabe cried in panic.

Fortunately for him, his mom decided to trust his instincts. She spoke via her watch phone to the head palace guard. "Prince Gideon is missing. Please have staff locate him immediately."

Conversation stopped as certain of the guests overheard the queen's words. She excused herself, saying something along the lines of her son loving to play hide and seek. Her guests nodded in understanding as the queen walked back into the palace with Gabe. Kids resumed playing, and the adults resumed talking and drinking.

The head palace guard was waiting for her. "Your Majesty, I have every available guard looking, and I've requested that the head of palace staff have his personnel look as well."

"You can't see him through the cameras?" the queen asked.

"We didn't see him come in on the cameras at all," the head palace guard replied, his brow furrowed, causing the queen to grow nervous.

Gabe looked at the guard. "We know how to get through the palace without being seen by the cameras."

The head palace guard nodded and knelt. "Is that so? Would you like to show me?"

Instead of replying, Gabe took a complicated route through the west side of the palace until he reached a small outdoor garden. He ran behind a large bush, and there he found his brother.

Gideon lay non-responsive on the ground. The queen called for help via her watch phone, and two doctors and several medical assistants came within minutes. The more senior doctor, the chief physician, did a quick look over the prince.

"His face is big," Gabe said.

The doctor nodded and looked inside Gideon's mouth. She then took a thick yellow pen and injected something into Gideon's right thigh. Gideon moaned almost inaudibly.

The doctor spoke to the queen. "I'm going to give him another shot, but we need to get him to a hospital right away. He was exposed to something to which he's allergic."

So, the party ended rather abruptly, the king came home right away, and Prince Gideon spent a week getting treated and recovering in the hospital. Prince Gabriel was taken every day to visit his brother and was generally mopey, weepy, and whiny when he had to leave the hospital to come home to the palace. The king and queen felt almost hysterical relief at the tragedy that was so nearly averted. Despite repeated tests, no doctor could determine what substance caused the prince's reaction. Gideon came away from the incident with a stronger appreciation for his brother, and he thought the reverse was true as well.

At that moment, Gideon's twin sense was raging loudly that his brother was feeling worse than he let on. He took a quick glance at Luke and James, who both were looking at Gabe, and gave a muffled sigh, his fingers drumming against his restless legs as he looked out the window. He knew that distant acquaintances or strangers often had trouble telling him and Gabe apart on looks alone, but they soon learned to identify Gideon by his constant movement. His parents could not cajole or beat him out of the habit, so they eventually gave up trying to change something so central to his character.

Gideon found it interesting that some people had such difficulty discerning the physical differences between him and Gabe. They were fraternal twins, not identical. While they were both a touch over six feet, tall for Seahorse, his brother—to Gideon's great annoyance—was about a quarter of an inch taller. Gideon was left-handed while his brother was right-handed. Gideon was a little thicker than Gabe. They both had bronzed skin, black almond-shaped eyes, long noses, medium lips, chiseled cheekbones, and closely cropped black hair. While the media generally described him and Gabe as handsome, Gideon was not so vain as not to understand a royal title and wealth often made one more handsome than he was in reality. Still, he thought he and Gabe did possess a certain elegant and approachable demeanor that made others enjoy their presence.

Looking at them after the fight, however, even those who knew them well would have trouble telling them apart, for Gideon, the loser of the last match, had the upright demeanor of the winner while Gabe, the winner, had the demeanor of one defeated.

Because The Red Palace was built on the side of a mountain, there were only two drives: one for arrivals to the palace and the other for departures from the palace. The drives were artfully landscaped on the sides but filled with twists and turns that made it impossible to drive with any real speed. Of course, there were emergency entrances and exits, some secret and some known.

Gideon knew, however, that his parents would not want the attention that would come with any use of an emergency entrance; otherwise, they would have had Gabe examined at the arena. It would not do for Seahorse's citizens to think there was anything amiss with Gabe's health. Gideon would just have to endure the long drive up the mountain to the palace. He would converse privately with his brother once they were there.

Gideon was relieved when the limousine finally pulled up to the palace and the Royal Snitches exited the vehicle to confirm that the surroundings were safe. "Can you make it inside on your own?" he asked Gabe, who had woken up once they stopped.

On Gabe's nod, he exited the limo and walked a little slower than usual until he and Gabe were beyond the massive, intricately carved double doors and into the palace. Gideon wasn't surprised to be greeted by the chief physician and several assistants. They had brought a hospital bed and some other medical apparatus, presumably to escort Prince Gabriel to the infirmary.

"What is all this?" Gabe asked, looking genuinely confused.

The chief physician bowed slightly from the waist. "Your Royal Highness, congratulations on your impressive win today. Your parents were concerned for your health and requested that we greet you."

Gideon was glad his parents had arranged for his brother to be examined. Fortunately, the palace had its own medical staff who were subject to strict confidentiality agreements, the violation of which was considered treason and punishable by death.

"There is no way I'm getting on that bed," Gabe argued. "I am the Supreme Fighter Champion! Why not check out the loser over there?"

Gideon shot Gabe an incredulous look and then said, "Let's both go, and we'll see who is the most recovered from three rounds of fighting!"

"Gabe!" Gabe's pregnant wife, Lily, stood between the medical staff and the princes, a look of horror on her face. She hadn't attended the fighting because she spent about half the day on bed rest per her doctor's recommendation.

"Babe, don't stress yourself. I won!" Gabe smiled his charming smile, one that usually made Lily smile back, despite whatever disagreement they happened to be having. It didn't work this time.

"You won?" Lily said with her head tilted to the side and one hand on her hip. "That's what you consider to be the most important thing right now?"

Before Gabe could answer, the chief physician coughed discreetly and said, "Pardon the interruption, Princes and Princess, but I advise that we continue the conversation in the infirmary."

"Fine," Gabe began, "but there is no way I'm lying in that bed like some sort of invalid. I'll wa—"

Before he could finish, Gabe collapsed and would have fallen to the floor if not for the medical assistants who grabbed him before he hit the floor. Lily screamed and then fell to her knees with her hand clutching her stomach. Another medical assistant went to assist her.

Gideon followed the mad dash to the infirmary, yelling at the Royal Snitches to update his parents. Minutes later, he stood outside the closed infirmary doors per the chief physician's request that he wait until they were done examining both patients.

In frustration, Gideon banged his left fist on the wall closest to the doors. Feeling drained and frustrated, he turned and leaned against the wall, eyes closed and arms crossed as he replayed the events of the day in his head, wondering what Gabe's symptoms could mean. He sighed as he heard footsteps and straightened his posture. His parents had arrived.

"What has happened?" the queen exclaimed, hurrying forward, her expression worried.

Her husband matched her pace, his expression grave. He looked at his son with a message which Gideon understood.

Gideon shook his head in response. "Gabe wasn't feeling well at the match, and Lily was worried about Gabe. They want to check them both out, just to make sure everything is ok."

"Yes, he has probably just been pushing himself too hard. I'm sure he will recover soon," his mother said, hugging herself. Gideon noticed that his mother said nothing about Lily or the baby.

Her husband, normally not one for public displays of affection, put his arm around her in comfort.

His father made a call to the head of palace staff and indicated that the family should not be disturbed while they waited. They sat on the padded benches in the waiting area outside the infirmary. The waiting area was lovely with the walls painted a light blush color and decorated with small pictures of plants and flowers native to the island. The coffee and side tables were topped with an array of pale roses in deference to the queen's edict that every room in The Red Palace have fresh flowers. If one wanted to catch up on news or be entertained, discreet tablets were available in small cubbyholes with sliding doors built right underneath the circular top of the coffee table.

Gideon failed to see any of these charming details. Instead, he sat unseeing, expecting word any moment, but no word came as a minute became an hour and then hours. Medical personnel would periodically come to and from with a deferential nod to him and his parents, all with the same line about testing. About hour three, the cheerful tone of the staff seemed forced, and eye contact was even less than usual.

"What is wrong with these people?" the queen exclaimed as she got up and paced. "I should fire all of them for incompetence."

"Jasmine," the king began, "I can't . . . let's not dissolve into histrionics. Gabe and Lily need us to be strong."

"No, Gabe needs us to be strong. Lily is just a social climber who has brought nothing of value to this family," the queen said. "I don't know why you didn't stop that wedding."

Both Gideon and his father put their heads in their hands as they waited for the queen to go on another tirade about Lily. She made no secret of the fact that she didn't like her.

After moments of silence, Gideon hesitantly raised his eyes and noticed that his father's expression was more tired and grave than usual, his lips a bloodless thin line and his skin chalky underneath the bronze color. As he watched his father, Gideon saw him close his eyes and pray silently.

His father was Christian, and his mother was Buddhist. Because of their father, both Gideon and his brother were Christians, but to Gideon, the rituals of church had no meaning. Church was just another royal duty that had to be done. Gideon knew that his father, however, strongly believed in his faith. As he watched his father pray and his mother pace, he felt like a ship without an anchor, incredibly tired and shaky.

Instead of continuing her tirade against Lily, Queen Jasmine sat beside her husband and leaned against him, her hands held tightly together. Gideon thought his mother let her pride get the better of her. She had a large circle of friends, many with eligible daughters. Before Gabe's marriage to Lily, Queen Jasmine loved to talk about her "ideal" daughter-in-law. She loved, even more, watching her friends prod their daughters into meeting this ideal. Gideon observed her antics with detached amusement. It wasn't unusual on the island for parents to actively assist their children in finding a spouse. However, the queen acted as though she had the final say about Gabe's bride. She planned to get Gabe married off first, and then Gideon.

When Gabe was twenty, she had narrowed the list of suitable brides to three and planned to talk with Gabe about them when he returned home on break from university. Much to her dismay, Gabe returned home expounding at length on the beauty of the heretofore unknown Lily.

IT WAS JUST COINCIDENCE, Gideon thought as he continued to wait with his parents, that he and Gabe met Lily their junior year at university, when the brothers were twenty and Lily was twenty-three. The brothers attended college abroad in London, where Lily had been raised from birth by her aunt. Lily's father had taken off when her mother announced the pregnancy, and her mother had died giving birth to her. Like her aunt, Lily was a nurse. At the time she met the twins, she had a master's degree in nursing and was well-regarded in the private hospital where she worked.

Gideon and his brother had needed a few routine vaccinations to remain in London, and Lily was the nurse who administered them. After they got to know her, Lily told them that the night before they met her, she had been assigned the night rotation from midnight until eight in the morning.

"You were?" Gabe had asked before he burst into laughter with Gideon. By then, the twins knew Lily well enough to know that anything less than eight hours of beauty sleep left her quite irritated.

"It's not funny. By eight, I was so exhausted I just wanted to cry," Lily exclaimed. "And then, to make matters worse, the eight o'clock nurse didn't show up, so I had to work even longer. It's a wonder I even gave you the right shots. At least, I hope I did." Lily's brow furrowed as she tried to remember.

"Don't worry about it," Gabe said. "I'm sure you gave us the right vaccinations." Gideon wasn't so sure, but he figured that thought was better unexpressed. Gabe was completely, utterly in love with Lily. He had shared with Gideon how he had become interested in her and maneuvered their first date.

According to Gabe, when he came in the private hospital late that morning with Gideon and their security detail, he would never have thought that he expected a certain amount of fawning over his title, well-honed physique, and impeccable tailoring. If one had even dared to imply that he was that vain, he would have expounded at length on the weight of his future responsibilities and his duty to always put the welfare of Seahorse Island first above all. Still, he admitted to Gideon that what drew him initially to Lily was her total lack of deference and her ability to treat him the same as everyone else.

Gabe told Gideon that Lily had laughed when he mentioned her ability to be unfazed by his status. She later shared with Gabe that she was normally a little star struck by some of the more famous patients that visited the private hospital where she worked, even though she was professional enough not to show it. But when she met the twins for the first time, she had been on her feet for almost the entire length of her extended shift. All she could focus on was the thirty-minute countdown to noon when the replacement was due to show up.

She vaccinated Gideon first and then Gabe, with their security detail present. After she vaccinated Gabe and gave him instructions for what to do should he experience side effects, Lily didn't process his request to perhaps go out for coffee correctly. She thought he asked for coffee, so she requested from the hospital's concierge staff that coffee—dark brew, cream but no sugar—be delivered right away to Prince Gabriel. She missed the smirk on Gideon's face and Gabe's answering scowl. The security detail pretended they saw nothing.

When Gabe made it back to his apartment on the River Thames in London, he still carried the cup of coffee, which he stared at for a while. Finally, he concluded to Gideon that he wanted to know the dark-haired nurse better. She made him curious. He came up with various plausible side effects from the vaccines and went back to the hospital a few days later. As luck would have it, Lily was on the day shift, and she was in a more conversational mood.

"Are you available for dinner tonight?" Gabe asked Lily as his visit concluded.

Lily smiled regretfully. "I'm so sorry, but the hospital has a strict policy about not going out with patients. Otherwise, I would love to go out for dinner."

"Well, what time do you go for your coffee break?" Gabe asked.

"Around noon?" she answered with a question in her voice.

"At the place on the corner?" He followed up with his most charming smile.

"Perhaps the Coffee Bliss place a few blocks north," Lily answered with a small smile as she caught on.

A few "accidental" coffee dates later, Gabe knew Lily was the woman he wanted to marry. It took over a year to make that dream a reality. First, Lily had to be convinced that Gabe was dating her with serious intentions. Then Lily had to make the harder decision about whether she wanted to date Gabe and incur all that dating him entailed—lack of privacy, nosy media, learning a different way of life than the one for which she had trained so very hard, and dealing with potentially difficult in-laws. Gideon had never seen his brother put so much effort into courting a woman as he did with Lily. Gideon had stood with pride as the best man at Gabe and Lily's marriage ceremony.

The way his brother and Lily loved each other sometimes made Gideon wonder when he would find a woman to love that deeply. His secret relationship with Angel seemed pale in comparison. Sometimes he felt lonely, especially with his brother preoccupied with Lily, and Angel was always available. But she wasn't the one. He wanted the woman he would know for sure was for him. Angel wasn't her, but at least she helped him not be alone. He was supposed to meet her that evening, but it wouldn't be the first time he didn't show. He figured he would connect with her on another night, once this situation with his brother had been straightened out.

THE CHIEF PHYSICIAN FINALLY APPEARED. Instead of coming through the infirmary doors, however, her image appeared on the VCD—Visual Communication Device—that had been hidden behind a wall panel. The doctor wore a closed expression. Gideon feared for what was to come next as he stood with his parents to hear the doctor's words. The physician bowed her head slightly on the screen.

"Your Highness, my sincere apologies for the long wait," the physician began.

"Please tell me; how are my son and his family?" the king requested.

"Why are you on the screen and not out here?" the queen asked.

After a slight pause, the physician said, "Let me start with the baby. He has a strong heartbeat. His mother did experience premature labor, which we were able to stop. We can monitor that—"

"What about my son?" Gideon's mother interjected, impatient.

3

EDEN, SCHOOL DAYS

I jerked awake the next morning, my muscles still tense. For a moment, I lay in a confused panic, wondering why the ceiling was so low and dingy. Then I remembered how I came to be in a room so very different from my own.

I sat up and grasped my knees, gasping as the motion caused pain to start again. My arms were still sore from being suspended, and the parts of me that had been hit were bruised and painful to the slightest touch. There was no mirror in the room, so I didn't have an idea of how terrible my face looked. The clock in the room said it was 4:30. I was no less confused this morning than I was the night before.

I remembered reading in church about Abraham's willingness to sacrifice his son Isaac and thinking with confidence that my mother or father would never sacrifice me for God or man. *They would go to hell first*, I'd thought, certain I was loved, that I was the sun that radiated life in my neat little world. My mind understood the need to get away from Inspector Brown, but my spirit could not accept that my parents would arrange for so brutal an arrangement. Anger rose within me like ocean waves. My body shook as I tried to contain the waves like a dam. I thought to pray but couldn't find the words. Instead, I thought about my new school.

The woman who greeted my arrival last night said her name was Mrs. Stout and that I was at the Joseph Hyde School for Exceptional Girls. Something about the way she said the word "exceptional" made me think she was mocking me, but I couldn't trust my own impressions at that point. She walked determinedly up the stairs to the room in which I was to sleep, explaining that breakfast was served at 8 a.m. sharp and that my orientation would be right after breakfast with Mrs. Grey. She slammed the door shut on her way out.

My room held a small closet with several changes of the school's uniform: a gray-white-and-black plaid jumper dress, black tights, black lace-up shoes, a long-sleeved white shirt to go underneath the dress, and a black-buttoned sweater for cold days. I felt depressed at the lack of color. There were also underwear and two long gray nightgowns. My skin itched from the nightgown I'd put on last night.

The surprising thing was the school logo: a mythical seahorse with the body of a horse covered in scales, elegant fins instead of hooves, and a luxurious mane of thick curly hair. The logo was on all the clothes, even the underwear. I shook my head briefly at the illogic of putting a logo someplace where no one would ever see. All the clothes were in my size, giving credence to Mrs. Stout's statement that my parents had arranged my placement at this school for "exceptional" girls.

If I stood in the center of the room with my arms straight out on both sides, I could almost touch the walls. The floor was brownish, and the walls were a dingy beige color. There was a small window with decorative wrought iron black bars. I could only open the window to circulate air; I couldn't lean out. I didn't see any fire stairs.

Still, the room had a plus. It gave me a better view of the campus than a room facing away from the school would have. The center of campus was laid out in a cross shape: a walkway going east and west, bisected in the middle by a walkway going north and south. The walkways were layered with attractive red brick and lined on all sides by beautiful shady trees. The lawns surrounding the walkways were still vibrant emerald, and a few benches loitered here and there.

No one was out and about just yet. It was that fragile time between night ending and day beginning. Each walkway led to one of four large buildings, each made with grimy Greystone facades and bricked sides, with few decorative touches. Each building seemed to be about five floors, with the top floor having some attic rooms with slanted roofs like the room I had been assigned. I felt hemmed in, even as I slept.

Around a quarter to seven, just when I thought I should start getting ready for the day, I heard a quiet tapping at my door. I stared at the door in surprise for a moment before opening it a sliver. Two faces looked back at me, one avidly curious. The faces belonged to two girls who looked about my age. I opened the door a little wider.

"Oh no! You look terrible!" said the tall, gangly girl with green eyes. Her hair was bright red and pulled back into a tight bun. Her face was covered with freckles, and there was a little gap between her top front teeth.

She pushed the door open and stepped in. "Giovanni must have been in a worse mood than usual. How are you? Does it hurt badly?"

She looked at me so sympathetically and warmly that my eyes started to tear up. I blinked back the tears. I didn't know her. Come to think of it, before being captured, I hadn't spoken to anyone who hadn't been introduced to me by my parents. So, I didn't say anything and just stared at the two girls, chewing my bottom lip indecisively.

"Well, I'm Kaitlyn, and doom-and-gloom over there is Bethany." Kaitlyn sat on the floor and looked at me expectantly. The other girl, presumably Bethany, sat as well. Her skin was pale ivory, and her blue-black hair was also pulled back into a tight bun. She frowned slightly and fiddled with a piece of red yarn in her hand.

Not knowing what else to do, I sat down on the floor as well, wincing slightly as I did so. "I'm Eden," I said. "Who is Giovanni?"

"Someone to avoid," Bethany replied.

"He only captures us," Kaitlyn said. "Once we're here, he doesn't have much to do with us. Just remember to follow the rules." She shrugged her shoulders.

I nodded, even though I didn't really understand.

"How old are you?" Kaitlyn asked. "I just turned fourteen in August and Bethany—"

"I can speak," Bethany interrupted. "I'm fourteen too. I assume you're the same age since your room is between Kaitlyn's and mine."

"Well, I'm thirteen," I said, "but I will be fourteen in October. I'm from Sunny City, New Jersey. Where are you from?"

"You're only thirteen!" Bethany exclaimed, looking totally discomfited. "This is high school, not junior high." Her tone made it seem like a complaint. She looked away from me and started biting her nails. They already looked well-bitten.

"Don't worry about Bethany," Kaitlyn said. "She's always PMSing."

I laughed from surprise or shock. I didn't know. Generally, one didn't talk about private things.

Bethany just rolled her eyes at Kaitlyn and stuck out her tongue. We all laughed at her antics and continued talking about nothing of consequence. I was dying to ask about their families and why they were at the school. I was trying to think of a safe question to ask when I heard Bethany gasp.

"You have to get dressed now," she said. The other girl was already opening the closet and pulling out clothes. I looked at the clock. The time was 7:53. I remembered that Mrs. Stout had said breakfast was served at eight sharp. Bethany and Kaitlyn were already dressed in their uniforms.

I hurriedly put on my clothes under my nightgown. The other two girls looked me with puzzled expressions. When I was fully dressed and had hung up the nightgown, Kaitlyn took a comb and tried to get it through my kinky, unruly hair, but the comb just snapped in half. That stopped her administrations momentarily, but then she just yanked my hair back into a big ponytail with the ends tucked under and declared me done. Bethany made the bed with quick, abrupt efficiency.

There was a slight creaking sound, and the girls hissed, "She's coming." In three seconds, they were gone.

I heard Mrs. Stout's hard gait. When she arrived at my open door, she took in my neat appearance. Her lips thinned in displeasure. She glanced around the room, and then I saw her eyes get a sudden gleam which made my stomach clench and my bowels get a little looser. She was a predator who had spotted a weakness.

"Mrs. Stout, you're wanted at the Jasmine House," said a stern voice, surprising us both. Mrs. Stout turn around, her displeasure obvious.

"I work at the Jade Vine House. This house." She practically bit the words out.

"Not anymore, you don't. Mr. Hyde says you've been transferred to the Jasmine House." This statement came from a woman practically half the size of Mrs. Stout. She was pale white with salt-and-pepper hair cut short and gray eyes that looked hard as flint. Deep grooves bracketed her mouth, and lines radiated from her eyes. She wore a tailored navy skirt, with nude hose, navy flats, and an ivory blouse with a pin decorated with a flower at her collar.

"Why did I get transferred?" asked Mrs. Stout, one plump hand on a bulging hip. Her eyes were hard.

"Why, I have no idea. Why don't you ask him?" the other lady replied. "Now, if you'll excuse me, I have a house to run."

I glanced at Mrs. Stout. Her hands were clenched into fists. I had no doubt that if she thought she could get away with it, she would've physically assaulted the smaller woman. I shuddered a little at the thought. After a tension-fraught silence, she stepped around and stomped down the steps. I could feel a tension headache developing.

The other woman spoke, "Good morning, Miss Edwards. I'm Mrs. Flint. I'm now the head of the Jade Vine House at the school. You'll learn all about the different houses and school rules at orientation. I won't bore you with the details now. How was your first night?"

Now, how was I supposed to answer that question? I struggled to find an answer that wouldn't offend.

"It was fine, ma'am," I eventually managed to say, but it came out more like a question than an answer.

"Really?" she queried, one black eyebrow raised. "We'll talk more later. You'd better get down to the dining hall."

"Yes, ma'am," I replied, and she walked on. I wondered what was at the end of the long hallway, and then I belatedly realized I didn't know where to find the dining hall. I hurried down the stairs, figuring my nose would lead me in the right direction. I ran into Bethany and Kaitlyn at the bottom of the stairs where Kaitlyn was retying her shoelaces and Bethany was both tapping her foot in impatience and biting her nails.

"Good, you're here," Kaitlyn said. "What did Mrs. Stout say?"

"Nothing to me. Mrs. Flint told her she got moved to one of the other houses, the Jasmine House," I replied.

Both Kaitlyn and Bethany looked at me with wide eyes, and then Kaitlyn laughed. "Well, what do you know. Mrs. Stout is out."

I thought I saw a small smile by Bethany, but it was so fleeting I could have been imagining things. I wondered why it was so great that Mrs. Stout was out.

"Let's talk later," Bethany whispered.

We had arrived at the dining hall. The smell of hot food made my stomach realize it had not eaten in a while. At the same time, I felt nervous when all heads turned toward the three of us. I lowered my gaze and let Kaitlyn and Bethany hurry me over to one of the tables.

There were two long tables parallel to each other which were packed with girls, maybe forty or so at each table. They were all quiet and sitting with their backs straight, looking composed. There was a third table on the other side of the entryway to the dining hall which sat on some sort of raised platform. It seemed to be where the adults sat. The wall behind the adults' table had three ceiling-to-floor posters of the school logo, the shiny seahorse with mesmerizing metallic colors and hair a glossy blue-black against swirling sea-greens and blues. The image was surprisingly hard to look away from. The center of the rug and ceiling had duller replications of the seahorse in their respective centers, surrounded by interlocking patterns of black, gray, and white squares. The wall that faced the outside of the building had four sets of slender side-by-side heavy black doors that were open so fresh air floated through. I could see the greenery outside.

I tried not to let my nervousness show as I looked around. The girls at the other table seemed slightly older than the girls at my table. Grandmotherly-looking ladies in uniform black knit dresses served us a breakfast of freshly squeezed orange juice, spinach cheese omelets, cubed potatoes, red grapes, and buttered whole wheat toast. After Mrs.

Flint said grace, everyone started eating and talking. The food was delicious in my mouth but settled uneasily in my stomach.

These girls were not like the girls I knew. They seemed to be without flaw. There were no pimples, braces, or awkward hairstyles. They gleamed with something I did not have. They were also polite. No one stared unduly long at my bruised face. If anything, the glances were sympathetic, but no one seemed surprised.

At home, everyone would have exclaimed in dismay and offered ice packs or something. I felt homesick for the comfort of knowing I belonged, that my world was settled. I was not sure I could ever possibly fit in here. And something tugged at the back of my mind, something else that worried me, but I couldn't bring it to the forefront of my mind, it being so crowded already with worries.

A bell rang, announcing the end of breakfast. Mrs. Flint stood to make announcements.

"Good day, ladies," she began.

"Good day, Mrs. Flint," everyone responded except me, but I hoped no one noticed my mistake.

"Mrs. Stout will be working with the Jasmine House from now on and will no longer be in the Jade Vine House. Unfortunately, we were not able to have a proper goodbye party for Mrs. Stout, as she needed to start right away at her new house," Mrs. Flint continued. I noticed a few of the girls seemed to be fighting smiles. No one seemed sad she had moved on.

"Also, I would like to announce that Eden Edwina Edwards has joined us today. Eden is a first-year student. Please give her a warm welcome."

Everyone clapped and smiled at me. I felt my cheeks flush and my throat constrict as I smiled back.

Another bell rang, and the girls around me began to get up to go to their first class. On her way out, Kaitlyn whispered that she and Bethany would try to catch up with me during the free hour. I nodded in agreement, even though I didn't know what time free hour started.

As I tried to figure out how to find the Mrs. Grey with whom I was supposed to have orientation, I saw one of the few remaining teachers stand and walk over to me. She seemed younger than the other teachers. Her light tan skin was still smooth, and her demeanor was less stern than the others.

"You must be Eden," she said, smiling and holding out her hand for me to shake. Her voice had a slight accent which I couldn't place.

"Yes, ma'am," I replied, surprising myself by smiling back.

"I'm Mrs. Grey. Let's go to my office, and we'll see what needs to be done."

Her office was larger than I expected, with space for a small round table, bookshelves on one wall, and a warm chocolate leather sofa. There was a tall, clear vase of pink roses on her desk and a round, squat vase of yellow roses on the table. Pictures and drawings of flowers had been framed and hung here and there.

Instead of sitting at her desk, Mrs. Grey indicated that we should sit at the round table. Mrs. Grey sat with her legs crossed and her upper body leaning forward, placing a small electronic notepad on the table.

"Eden," she began, "first, welcome to our lovely school. I know that the journey here is always miserable, but it is for the best, is it not?"

I nodded in confused agreement. How was this arrangement for the best?

Mrs. Grey smiled at me and picked up the electronic notepad. While she was engaged with it, I looked around her office, noticing how nicely decorated it was in comparison to my room. I wondered if the teachers lived on campus and what their rooms were like. I hoped my thoughts were not envious.

"I know," Mrs. Grey said, startling me. I hadn't been aware she was observing me. "Your rooms are dreary. But the school feels the Spartan rooms make you girls more appreciative of your new homes once you leave the school."

"Don't we go back home?" I asked, tilting my head to the side.

Mrs. Grey's fingers started tapping the table. "Eden, you do understand what we do at this school, don't you?" she asked.

It's a school. It's not that hard to figure out. "You educate girls so they can be in the ten percent who can attend a university," I stated, but with a questioning lilt at the end, rethinking my assumption as I spoke it.

Mrs. Grey just looked at me for a moment and then asked, "Is that what you'd like to do, go to a university?"

"Yes, ma'am. I would like to major in world languages," I replied. Learning new languages was not hard for me, and I enjoyed reading books in their original language if I could. I had always imagined doing missionary work when I grew up, and I knew speaking multiple languages would be helpful.

"Ok. I see you have some misunderstandings," said Mrs. Grey. "You are correct that only girls who score in the top ten percent on the college entrance exam can attend the women universities. All the other girls must be matched by their pastor if they haven't found someone on their own. Why do you want to be in the ten percent who don't have to be married by eighteen?"

"I would like to do missionary work."

Mrs. Grey just continued looking at me, waiting for me to expound. I didn't. I just looked down at my hands.

"Do you want to be married?" Mrs. Grey asked.

"Of course," I said, looking back up.

"You do know that to take the entrance exam, a woman has to be sponsored by a home inspector and someone from their city or town council?" she asked me gently.

I did not know this. "Are you sure? I thought everyone just did the test," I said, not wanting to believe that my path to college could be hindered by the same Inspector Brown that was the reason for my presence here. But I realized that wasn't the most important issue. "Why don't we go home after we leave here? Wouldn't my family want me back home?" I asked.

"Eden, the reason you were very publicly kidnapped in broad daylight was to get you out of the clutches of your chief home inspector without suspicion being cast on your family. Your Aunt Adeline is paying for your education with us." Mrs. Grey paused and then continued. "You are off the radar now, and that's a good thing. The bad news is that you will not be able to leave this campus for at least another four years. You will not see nor contact your family during this time. All electronic communications are monitored. Do you understand?" she asked.

I couldn't speak for a moment. I wanted to throw myself on the floor and have a big temper tantrum, something I was never allowed to do at home. Mrs. Grey's calm and sympathetic gaze just made me even angrier. I knew I had to rein in my emotions. I clenched my fists and jaw tight to hold everything in.

Finally, when I thought I could speak civilly, I said, "My mom said they—my parents—would visit me." The quiver in my voice was slight, but I was sure Mrs. Grey noticed. I also remembered that my mom said no men were allowed at the school, yet Giovanni seemed to be an accepted presence.

"Yes, well, the school did a little digging into your situation, and we discussed with your parents that no contact would be better for your safety. They agreed." Mrs. Grey did not look at me as she delivered this news.

The dam inside of me burst. I put my face in my hands and cried. Mrs. Grey sat patiently, and when my tears subsided, she handed me some delicately scented tissues. The scent made my nose twitch, and I started sneezing. Eventually, I recovered myself and looked at Mrs. Grey with watery eyes. I pressed my lips together firmly to keep from blubbering.

"I know this situation seems pretty dire, but what are your alternatives? If you stayed at home, your virtue would be taken by Inspector Brown, you'd get blamed for it, and your parents would have to kick you out of their home. You would eventually end up in Untouchable City. You can't go to university. No one would sponsor you."

My cheeks burned at her words. I hated how cavalierly she'd laid out my lack of options.

"But let's look on the bright side," she continued. "You're blessed to have a family who pulled every string and every dollar they had to get you into our school. We consider ourselves a high school, which means you typically need to be fourteen to start, but based on your academic record, we think you can start now. You've only missed a little over a week of the school year. The school hopes that at the end of your four years here you will get married. If that happens, we will help you put together a good cover story for the last four years. If you are so unfortunate as to not secure a marriage proposal, then you will be placed as a companion to men who desire your company. This school graduates soon-to-be wives or companions. Not one of our graduates in our entire history has ever gone on to university. Ninety-five percent do get married, so it's not a bad deal. And if your husband allows, you will finally get to see your family again," she finished.

"How can I get married if I never leave the campus? Are there boys here?" I asked, thinking the question was stupid as soon as I asked. I couldn't see my family for four years, and I was asking about boys?

"No, the marriages are arranged. The price for the arrangement is about two hundred thousand dollars plus expenses, so the men who marry our graduates are wealthy, if not rich. We only take girls for whom we are confident we can place in marriage. We already have several interested parties for you. All you have to do is study hard and do well, and everything should fall into place."

"How would they know about me?" I asked, confused.

Mrs. Grey pushed a folder across the table to me. I opened it, to see a picture of myself sitting on a blanket at Sunny City Gardens while reading a book. There was short bio with my height, weight, blood type, and other information. I was described as a shy Christian girl.

I wasn't sure I could contain my breakfast. My tension headache was throbbing, my lips pressed tight together, and I struggled not to embarrass myself any further.

"Tuition is only fifty thousand dollars for your entire four years with us. However, the cost per student is thirty-eight thousand per year, so the two hundred thousand dollars is how we recoup our cost. Once we receive the two hundred thousand dollars for you, we will reimburse your aunt for the tuition she paid."

"What if I fail my courses?" I asked.

"Then there's no reimbursement," Mrs. Grey replied.

"I meant, what happens to me if I fail? Do I get sent home?"

"Actually, no. If you fail, there are no good options. You would be sent to one of the other houses," Mrs. Grey replied. "However, I am sure you will do wonderfully well with us. There are a number of rules, and all of them are included in your orientation folder." She pushed a glossy maroon folder across the table to me. "We expect all the Jade Vine girls to behave with discretion, decorum, self-respect, and exemplary behavior. Any breach of the rules can be grounds for expulsion from the house and reassignment to another house. Do you understand?"

"Not really. If I were to be expelled, why would I be sent to another house? Wouldn't I just go home?" I asked.

Mrs. Grey's smile tightened as she replied, "The Jade Vine House is the best house, the best option for girls like you. The other houses are strictly to prepare girls to become companions. Under no circumstances are you to associate with or speak to girls from those houses. The consequences for doing so are severe. They know, of course, not to speak to you as well."

I didn't know how to respond, so I just sat in shocked silence.

Mrs. Grey continued, "With respect to not speaking, it is also advised that you not speak of where you are from. The main asset of this school, besides you girls, is that its existence and location are completely secret from most. The teachers who work here are all sworn to secrecy. This is all, of course, to give you girls a new start in life. You can't have a new life if you let everyone know all the details of your old life. Do you understand?"

I nodded, thinking I had already told Bethany and Kaitlyn I was from Sunny City. *Would that cause a problem?* I wondered.

"Of course, I'm sure you will do well," Mrs. Grey continued. "You'll take Domestic Arts, The Art of Conversation, History, Household Budgeting, English, French, and Spanish. Domestic Arts is a two-hour course every day, Monday through Friday. The rest of the courses are between sixty and ninety minutes. You take the Art of Conversation on Saturday. Every other Saturday, you visit with a beauty specialist to help you learn the art of always looking your best. Quiet Bible study time is from five to six every evening."

"We don't go to a church?" I asked, my mind not focused on the class list.

"It's against the law for women to teach biblical principles but not against the law for you to read the Bible yourself. Eden," Mrs. Grey continued with just a hint of impatience, "we've been doing this for years. Trust me; we know what we're doing." She gave me a confident smile.

Mrs. Grey went to her desk and handed me an electronic notepad for taking notes. "The notepad is already set up with the books you'll need for class. You can start tomorrow. If you need any more supplies, please don't hesitate to ask me. Right now, I want you to go to the infirmary and have your bruises looked at. Mrs. Stout and her son, Giovanni, can be a little heavy-handed at times, yes?"

When I slowly nodded, she continued. "Lunch is optional today, but starting at dinner, you must attend every meal unless you're excused by the nurse."

At the infirmary, a brisk and efficient nurse applied salve to the bruises on my face, telling me I could apply it to other parts of my body myself, and gave me some medication to take for my headache. She offered her sofa if I wanted to take a nap.

I lay down more out of habit, as I was used to obeying. I didn't think I would sleep. I must have been more tired than I thought, because I woke up almost three hours later and urgently had to use the washroom.

After I was done, I noticed there was a full-length mirror on the back of the washroom door. My light-brown complexion stared back at me, the bruises from yesterday clearly visible. I had round cheeks that dimpled when I smiled, but I wasn't smiling. My eyes were slightly almond-shaped and dark, with flecks of amber that were only visible in good light. My blondish-brown, kinky-curly hair needed a good comb through, but I didn't have the energy for it. I was a little taller than average, and my chest was no longer pancake flat. My size 32B bra felt constricting.

I wanted to squeeze into a little genie bottle and go back in time. Everything seemed too disturbing. Why was I favored to live in the Jade Vine House when other girls weren't? I knew from overheard whispered conversations that companions were considered little better than dirt and that the stain was permanent. No girl could better herself after being a companion. Without my aunt's money—or rather, her dead husband's money—would I be just like them? The firm ground I was used to standing on now felt like quicksand. Unmotivated to face the other girls at lunch, I went upstairs to my assigned room.

Looking out the window, I could see some of the girls from the other houses. They wore the same uniforms and polished veneer as the girls in the Jade Vine House, my house. But even from the fifth floor, I could see that they carried themselves with more tension. I remembered going with my mom once to donate clothes to a homeless shelter and noticing the wiry thinness on some of the women. It was less dieting and exercise and more living a hard life with no room for extras or dreaming. These girls had that sort of hardness. They were diamond-hard beautiful.

I had decided to lie down for a little while longer, when my eye spotted my jean fabric purse under the bed. I hadn't realized I still had it. Maybe that was what Mrs. Stout had glimpsed when her eyes got that unholy gleam.

I rummaged through it, trying to find vestiges of my old life. I found lip moisturizers, clear nail polish, items for monthly use, and a small envelope. I opened the envelope, to find a note. "We're so sorry. There was no other way. Pray and live well." The note was in my mother's handwriting. The envelope included her favorite necklace, which had a small golden cross embedded with diamond chips. I remembered my mother taking my purse briefly at Sunny City Gardens. I was glad for a note from her and put the necklace on under my shirt. I didn't want it to get taken away.

But what else had she said? She had put pocket money in my purse. I looked and just saw the usual assortment of coins. I shrugged to myself, put the note back, and started to close the purse, when I saw that I had lipstick in my purse as well. Ruby Blush #12, my mom's favorite lipstick that she only used on special occasions since the color had been discontinued. I wondered why it was in my purse as I opened it up. Even though it was an extra-large tube for lipstick, there was so little left that I would've had to use a finger or a Q-tip to dig out enough to apply to my lips.

I twisted the bottom a little, and that's when I heard the slight crinkly sound of paper. I felt a shiver run through me as I continued to turn the bottom and revealed hidden cash. I hurriedly turned the knob the other way and put the top back on the lipstick. I closed my purse and put it on the top shelf in the closet. At least I wasn't in the middle of nowhere without funds. But, come to think of it, I really didn't know where the Joseph Hyde School for Exceptional Girls was located. There was no address or phone number on any of the school material Mrs. Grey had given me. There was just the school name.

Frustrated, I fell back on the bed. My mother had always advised me to live well. How could I live well when others were in situations that were shameful? If I had been used by Inspector Brown, I wouldn't have been able to recover and move on, even though it wouldn't have been my fault. This new arrangement, however, still made me feel dirty in some inexplicable way. I felt ashamed of my good fortune but relief that I wasn't in one of the other houses.

My feeling of relief made me feel ashamed again, and my head spun in a circle of relief and shame the rest of the day. That night, I dreamed I was at a great feast at my new house, the Jade Vine House. None of the girls wore uniforms but instead wore expensive sparkly jewelry and beautiful expensive gowns. I could smell the scent of lighted vanilla candles. The smoke from the candles twirled lazily upward. The men were in black tuxedos and their faces shadowed, but I could feel their maleness, even in the dream. Their delighted male laughter was interspersed with softer, lighter feminine laughter.

The dinner bell rang, and everyone moved to the crystal-and-linen-topped table. On top of the table lay a female form, covered mostly with a white sheet and surrounded by flowers. I looked at her face, and that was when I realized I was not a horrified guest at the party. I was the meal.

I woke up, sweating and gasping for air, the sheets twisted and damp. My heart was galloping so fast I put my hands over my chest as if to keep my heart from running away.

4

GIDEON, THE FRUIT OF SIN

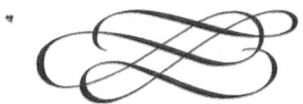

"*I* deeply regret to inform you that your son has tested positive for the *Denique sperma virus*."

Gideon watched his mother gasp and fall gracelessly back onto the padded bench. His father swayed as though hit by a strong wind.

"How is this possible?" the king asked as he looked at Gideon. "We never cut any corners while trying to keep that virus out."

The *Denique sperma virus* owed its nefarious existence to a bioterrorist named Dr. John Spike. Dr. Spike was a soft-spoken, mild-mannered madman. He thought most of the world's population should be wiped out, except for a select few who would represent a new world order based on reason.

To achieve such an inhuman goal, Mr. Spike bred mosquitoes in his private Peruvian lab to see if they could carry certain deadly strains of viruses. After years of soul-crushing failure, Dr. Spike believed he would never achieve his goal and burned down his lab. Unfortunately, a few of his lab mosquitoes got out of the burning toxic mass. Those mosquitoes carried a virus strain that induced high fevers, tremors, and vomiting. Those symptoms, however, while severe, were only temporary. The virus also caused severe and permanent impact to the reproductive health of those it infected. They either became sterile or had a ninety-nine percent chance of having offspring with severe birth defects.

As a result, most countries—if not all—made it a serious criminal offense for those affected by the virus to procreate. Parents had to have a reproductive license before they could procreate. Many women with licenses were also carriers for families impacted by the virus. The virus infested not just the usual suspects—tropical and subtropical areas—but even managed to thrive in some cold weather climates.

Seahorse Island had never encountered the virus. The island ran a highly aggressive mosquito abatement program. Some environmentalists and watchdog groups complained about the chemicals used by the island, claiming they were more toxic than the mosquitoes they were trying to wipe out. The spokesperson for the royal family noted that Seahorse Island was one of only seven places in the world where the *Denique sperma virus* had not taken root. Even Saved America was not spared by the virus. These factors doused water on the fire the complainants were trying to flame.

To be told on a day meant for celebration that the dreaded virus was now on Seahorse Island and had infected the royal family was horrific for Gideon. It was his job to oversee the mosquito abatement program. He had failed not just his family but his country as well.

For a long minute, Gideon tried to process this catastrophic turn of events as knife-like feelings of shame and fear bludgeoned through his normal sense of self. No wonder the chief physician appeared on the screen. The medical staff was now in quarantine. While the virus was primarily transmitted by mosquitoes, it could also be spread through contact with an infected person's blood.

Gideon felt sweat bead on his forehead as he looked at the stricken faces of his parents and thought about Gabe's grayish-blue face at their fight. He thought of Lily, the person who shared the most intimate contact with Gabe, and felt nauseous.

"Father, I'm not sure how the virus got on the island. After I check on Gabe, I will speak with the minister of health and follow the emergency plan for this event."

"Your mother and I will check on Gabe. You should go talk to the minister of health now. Consider this matter your most urgent priority," the king ordered Gideon with a hard stare before turning to speak to the chief physician.

Gideon clinched his jaw, nodding tightly, and left to follow his father's instructions.

"WHAT! THE *DENIQUE SPERMA VIRUS*!" The minister of health's hands shook slightly before he placed them on his lap. They were sitting in a small conference room to the side of Gideon's office. The minister had apparently been about to bed down for the night when he was summoned to the palace. Gideon knew from experience that Minister Kang was a conscientious and detail-oriented minister. But still, the virus had made its way to the island, and they needed to take immediate action to stop it.

"Yes, we have a confirmed case, so we need to follow the emergency procedures. We need to take all available measures—no shortcuts—to stop the spread. How it got onto the island, who has it or had it, and how to stop its spread. We need all of that information ASAP," Gideon replied without his usual politeness when speaking with the minister.

"I will pull my team together tonight and staff this matter on a twenty-four-hour basis per the emergency procedure. We will need to get in contact with the confirmed case right away. I am surprised my office was not informed. Where is the patient?" the minister asked.

Here Gideon paused. He wasn't sure that information should get out.

"Your Royal Highness, it is very important that we place Patient Zero in isolation, as well as anyone who may have had contact with the patient. We need to target around his or her communal home to kill any hidden pockets of mosquitoes." Here Minister Kang paused with a grimace. "We will also need to determine how this information should be communicated so as not to cause panic."

Gideon responded, "Communicate that the virus may—emphasis on *may*—have reached the island. Request that folks with any medical symptoms call in. All events should be canceled, and all businesses and schools are to be closed for the next few days. I will speak to my father about rescheduling the celebration for the fight."

Minister Kang opened his mouth and then closed it, but Gideon could almost hear the objections running through his mind.

"Do you have any members of your staff who are exceptional workers and discreet?" Gideon asked.

"What?" Minister Kang responded in a surprised voice, sitting up even straighter. "Yes, of course I do. Why do you ask?"

"I need a team assigned to The Red Palace." Gideon looked away. The minister of health did not readily respond, and the silence stretched out.

"I saw the match today with my daughter, Angel," the minister eventually spoke. "I suspected your brother was not well after the fight. How long has he been sick?"

"Three weeks," Gideon replied, wondering if the minister knew about his relationship with Angel. For such a conscientious professional, Minister Kang missed much as a father.

Minister Kang nodded his head as though confirming something and then stood up.

"I will follow your plan, Prince Gideon. Expect a team at the palace within an hour. The medical staff from the infirmary should stay in the infirmary until we can test them."

Gideon nodded and walked back over to his desk. He reached for his journal to write down his thoughts for all the avenues he would need to address with the virus situation. His assistants hated the habit, preferring that he use an electronic notepad. Writing helped him better remember his thoughts. However, before he could write, he needed the minister to leave. The minister had followed him and was standing in front of the desk with an uncomfortable look on his face.

"What is it?" Gideon asked impatiently.

"Has your brother been out of the country recently?" Minister Kang asked.

"No, he hasn't," replied Gideon. "The last time he left the island was a couple of months ago."

Minister Kang looked embarrassed and said, "Sir, it is unexpected that in three weeks no other cases have become known. Mosquitoes are rapid reproducers."

Gideon must have looked puzzled because Minister Kang abandoned the hints. "Sir, is it possible that your brother did not get the virus from a mosquito?"

"But how else would he get the virus?" Gideon asked, still confused.

"If he is the only one with symptoms after three weeks, it may be that he doesn't have the virus and was incorrectly diagnosed. Considering the quality of the palace medical staff, I think that option is unlikely. What is more likely on the probability scale is that the prince has the virus, but he didn't get it from a mosquito. Someone could have delivered it by placing it in hot liquid given to the prince or through an injection through his skin."

Gideon stood up in alarm. "But I thought it had to be blood-to-blood transmission if not directly from the mosquito."

"This is not well-known, but it is possible to make a dry version of the virus in a lab. Putting the dry version in liquid and heating it to a certain temperature would activate the virus, albeit for only a limited time—no longer than thirty minutes."

GIDEON SAT and watched his brother sleeping, his own eyes heavy with the need to sleep. His hair needed a trim and his clothes, usually immaculate, were rumpled. Gideon could smell that he needed a shower.

Minister Kang had confirmed that there were no other cases of the virus since Gabe had fallen ill. The only conclusion drawn for how Gabe had acquired the virus was that the transfer had been deliberately done by human hands. The frustrating thing for Gideon was that no one knew by whose hands the deed had been done. He wanted to scream and yell and hit something when both the minister of defense and the minister of health told him his brother's situation was a clear case of biowarfare. Gideon felt the desire boiling in himself to avenge the harm that had been done to his brother. He knew other countries frowned upon the island's liberal use of capital punishment, but Gideon knew he would recommend no less once this enemy was found.

Gideon ran his hand through his hair again. He replayed the weeks before his brother fell sick over and over in his mind. Earlier, he had looked through Gabe's calendar and tried to think of any persons he might have overlooked. The weeks leading up to the fight had been the slowest of the year for administrative and royal duties, but there were still quite a few meetings the brothers had to attend. Eventually, in frustration, Gideon had asked the defense ministry to follow up on every point of contact for both him and Gabe during the month before the fight. Nothing untoward was found.

Gideon clenched his fists together and rested his forehead on them. He felt wetness on his hands, and as he lifted his head, a single tear drop fell and splattered on his clenched fist. Shaking his head, he quite firmly wiped his hand down his face. He needed to sleep, but every time he closed his eyes, worries over the situation with his brother would cause his mind to spiral in an endless cycle of unanswerable questions. Maybe if he meditated, his mind and body would finally rest.

"Gideon." His brother spoke his name quietly, his eyes closed.

"How did you know it was me?" Gideon asked.

"Who else could it be? You smell like shit," his twin replied as he tried to lift himself up.

"Oh, look, the sick man talking big," Gideon replied as he helped Gabe sit up. "You are supposed to be lying down, resting."

Gabe looked at him like he wanted to refute his statement but then closed his eyes again as he asked, "What is happening?"

Gideon hesitated in answering. His brother was very ill. In just ten days, his body was noticeably thinner. The doctor said the recovery process would be slow. Until a day ago, Gabe had been in quarantine, as had all the medical staff who treated him. He decided to stick to safe conversations.

"Lily is fine. I actually think her stomach has gotten bigger." Gideon paused before continuing. "Other parts of her have gotten impressively larger as well."

"You are a complete ass," Gabe replied. "Once I recover from this virus, you know I will still be a better fighter than you."

"Seriously," Gideon retorted. "You want to go with that theory? If I hadn't gone easy on you, you would be . . ." Horrified that he had been about to say the word "dead," Gideon blanked on trying to come up with a more appropriate word.

"Look, I know I don't have just a regular virus. What's the impact on the island?" Gabe sounded worried. "They took away all my devices and my access to the net. All I can do is re-watch cartoons that weren't funny the first time we saw them as kids."

"The island is fine. You got the virus through biowarfare."

Gabe turned his head sharply to look at Gideon and then winced.

Gideon stood up. "Do you need me to get the nurse?"

"No, just tell me who did it," his brother croaked out.

Instead of immediately answering, Gideon poured a glass of water from the carafe on the table next to him and handed it to Gabe. "We don't know who did it, but I'm working on it."

Gabe said nothing in response to this news. He took one sip of water before handing the glass back to Gideon and closing his eyes. He was quiet for so long that Gideon thought he had fallen asleep. He wanted to ask his brother about any unusual occurrences over the last few weeks that could explain how the virus was administered. He would have to wait.

As Gideon walked silently out of the large infirmary room, Gabe said, "I'm sorry, brother."

Thinking his brother was talking about falling asleep, Gideon said, "It's ok." He closed the door quietly and left. It would be two years before he understood his brother's apology.

As Gideon left the infirmary, he ran into his grandmother. Her long white hair was loose instead of being pulled back into a bun, and she was dressed in a white cotton nightgown.

"Ya Ya, you are here to visit Gabe?"

His grandmother slowly nodded, and then her eyes filled with tears. She seemed stricken with grief.

Gideon sighed and hugged his grandmother. "Ya Ya, he's not dead. He will recover."

He was surprised when she pushed him away, her strength greater than he suspected.

"I warned you," she hissed in an accusing voice.

Gideon stared at her. He had never seen this side of his grandmother.

"I warned you," she said again, despairingly, the venom in her voice gone as her whole body slumped in disappointment.

"Ya Ya, I did ask the maintenance folks if they had any issues with snakes or if they'd seen any snakes. No one has seen anything," Gideon said, hoping to reassure her.

"You have eyes to see but do not see," his grandmother replied, turning to shuffle back to her personal rooms instead of visiting Gabe.

Gideon opened his mouth to ask her to explain but then felt exhaustion weigh heavily on him. He needed sleep more than another confusing conversation with his grandmother. He walked her quietly back to her rooms before going to his own suite. He lay down, fully clothed, and got his first full night of sleep since Gabe became ill.

THE NEXT DAY AROUND MIDAFTERNOON, a royal page stopped by Gideon's office to inform him that "the king" requested his presence immediately. A page only used his father's title if his father instructed them that the matter pertained to official business with respect to running the island. Gideon aborted the phone call he was about to make and headed over to his father's—the king's—office suite. His father's suite was not far from his own.

Upon arriving at his father's office, he was greeted rather abruptly by his father's royal assistant, Joseph Park. "Your father will be with you shortly."

Surprisingly, he didn't stand as he usually did upon greeting a member of the royal family. He didn't even look up. Gideon almost commented on his rudeness but decided to hold it in for now. Park had been his father's assistant since before Gideon was born and was a stickler for following all social courtesies. Gideon decided to assume Park was working urgently on something for the king.

After thirty minutes of waiting for his father, Gideon decided his time would be spent more productively in his office, getting work done and getting updates on the virus situation. As he moved to walk out of the waiting area of his father's office suite, however, Royal Assistant Park spoke.

"Your father specifically requested that you wait here until he is available."

Gideon nodded and paced a bit before sitting back down, his fingers and right leg continuing to bounce. He couldn't remember the last time his father made him wait for such a lengthy period. If something urgent came up requiring his father's immediate attention, he would just wave Gideon away and circle back when his schedule opened. Specifically making Gideon wait was something the king only did when he was extremely displeased.

Gideon stopped moving as he tried to think of any new thing that could have angered his father. Perhaps the king was very upset over his lack of progress in finding the virus culprit?

After Gideon had waited an hour, his father called him into his office. Gideon walked in and decided to go on the offense. "What have I done this time?" he said as he sat down, facing his father across the rather overlarge ornately carved desk.

"I did not give you permission to sit," his father said, ice dripping from each syllable.

"What?" Gideon asked, more surprised than dismayed.

His father just looked at him impassively. Gideon stood and waited to hear judgment on his yet unknown crime.

"How is Angel?" his father asked.

Gideon felt his stomach drop as he tried to keep his face as impassive as his father's.

"Minister Kang's daughter? She seems fine. Why do you ask?"

His father's hard eyes bored into him, and Gideon dropped his gaze first.

"Is her father upset?" Gideon asked, wondering how much he should admit to. "Is he—is he hoping I'll marry her?" Gideon felt his throat tighten at the thought.

"Minister Kang has resigned," his father said with a sigh.

"Why?" Gideon asked, even more bewildered than before.

"Angel was the person who delivered the virus to your brother," his father said.

Gideon could not comprehend his father's statement. "What are you talking about?" he asked. He could not imagine Angel with the intellectual capacity to even dream up such an idea.

His father shook his head at Gideon. "Angel assumed you would marry her. She figured if she made your brother sterile, then he would have only one heir, which would make any sons she had with you that much closer to the throne. I suppose she thought having such sons would increase her stature."

Gideon thoughts were scrambled. Angel was someone with whom he'd had a bit of fun, with no intention of marriage. He couldn't place her in any other category.

"But this doesn't seem like Angel," he said eventually.

"Or maybe this situation doesn't seem like the Angel you know," his father said, leaning back in his chair. "How well do you know Angel?"

"I—I—I know her somewhat well," Gideon finally stammered out, still standing.

"Really? Did you know she got this virus from the terrorist group Seven?" His father abruptly stood, picked up a glass paperweight from his desk, and threw it against the wall. It shattered into a thousand shards of glass. Gideon had never seen his father lose control.

"How could you do this?" his father asked him, breathing hard.

"But how?" Gideon asked, his mind too turmoiled to think in complete sentences.

His father started to speak and then paused and blew out a breath. "Through you," he replied.

"No, I never—" Gideon began. He stopped as his father shook his head at him in disappointment.

Gideon thought back to his time with Angel. She worked as the entertainment director at the Foreign Quarter's famous Merman Hotel. Gideon would frequently reserve the Royal Suite at the hotel for meetings. The suite included conference rooms, a sitting room, and a small-but-luxurious bedroom with a bath and small kitchenette. In the guise of going over details for his visits, Angel would visit him after his guests had departed.

He winced as he remembered their last conversation. They were getting ready to leave his suite and Angel was helping him adjust his tie.

She asked "Gideon, when can we do an official parents meeting?"

Gideon looked at her in shock. Angel still held his tie in her hands, and her gaze was painfully hopeful as she gazed up at him. The hope in her eyes almost repelled him.

He swallowed hard before he said, "I thought we agreed that this wasn't a serious relationship."

"We did," she agreed, looking down at the tie gripped tightly in her hands. "But I thought we'd come to care for each other." Her gaze rose to meet his, and he saw the glisten of tears in hers.

Could I be with her? he thought to himself. They had been friends since kindergarten. On the first family visit day for their kindergarten class, Angel had no one with her. She had stood with her eyes downcast, clutching her hands together, her hair in uneven pigtails. Her mother had died when Angel was two years old, and Angel's father was so focused on work that he forgot to mark the date on his calendar. As she stood in the corner of their classroom, some parents looked sideways at her and then whispered amongst themselves. Gideon could remember feeling bad for her, but he couldn't remember if it was him or Gabe who had invited her to their table. On that day, Angel ended up hanging out with him, his brother, and his mother. His mother showed unusual forbearance. She exclaimed over Angel's work just like she did with her boys.

Angel had remained their close friend until recently. With Gabe spending his time with Lily, Gideon found himself spending more time alone with Angel. On the night of Gabe's bachelor party at the Merman Hotel, Gideon had drunk more than he should've, and instead of going home, he spent the night at the hotel. Angel was on duty that night, and they had slid from an innocent friendship to a relationship that would be frowned upon were it known.

"Gideon," Angel said, interrupting his thoughts. Her grip on his tie was almost strangling him, and tears poured down her face. "You don't want to be with me?" she asked, her voice quavering.

With her one question, Gideon realized he didn't want to be with her in the way she was asking. He didn't want to marry her to make the relationship right. As feelings of guilt flooded him, he struggled to stay still. But he really couldn't look at her, or she would know the truth. He needed to find a way to end the relationship that didn't cause her pain.

"Let me think about it," he said, turning away from her and putting on his suit jacket.

When he turned back, Angel smiled at him and leaned over to kiss his cheek. As they walked to the door, he pondered the problem. So deep in thought was he that he bumped into Angel who had paused.

"Oh, I almost forgot. I left you a present." She walked over to the side table in the sitting room where she picked up two boxes, one wrapped in shiny black-and-gold-striped wrapping paper, the other in shiny green-and-gold-striped wrapping paper. Both boxes had a big gold bow on top.

"It's Ming tea, very rare. The green tea is for you, and the black tea is for your brother. I think the green tea has the better flavor, so that one's for you." She had held the boxes out to him with a charming smile.

"It was the tea," he said, gripping the chair in front of him as he looked at his father.

His father nodded. As he took in the full implications of his father's confirmation, Gideon clinched his fists to keep his body from shaking with shame and grief. Beads of sweat broke out on his forehead as he struggled to absorb that he was the cause of his brother's illness, the fact that his brother and Lily would never have any more children together, and that he had lost his father's love and respect. Despite his best efforts, his eyes filled with unshed tears, and a visible tremor went through his body.

"What will happen to Angel?" he asked.

"She will be executed, along with any member of the Seven that we can find."

"Execution . . ." Gideon was furious that Angel had used him for such a destructive plan, but he just couldn't picture her before the royal executioner, especially when he felt partially responsible for her actions. "Is there any—" He stopped speaking as his father stomped around the desk and grabbed Gideon by the shoulders.

"Only by grace did I not lose two sons, my only children. If Angel did not have her own plan of trying to marry you, who knows how much damage she could have done with Seven's resources. Did you really think I would show her mercy?"

Gideon shook his head.

"It makes me furious that that child sat in my kitchen and played with my children. Even your mother was nice to her. I feel doubly betrayed. She and all members of the Seven will be executed, no exceptions. We only have members of five cells instead of the entire seven, but as we find them, they will be executed."

Gideon nodded in a jerking motion.

"If it's any consolation, it appears that Angel did love you in a twisted sort of way." His father shook his head as he dropped his hands from Gideon's shoulders. "But as you can now see, her love was destructive. We found out from one of the men we captured that she used Seven to get the tea with the virus, promising them information from certain meetings at the Merman Hotel."

Gideon shook his head, confused. "But you said she thought—she thought I would marry her?"

"Ah, yes. She had a backup plan in case you didn't ask her. She was ready to blackmail you into marriage."

Gideon stood still as he tried to process his father's words.

"Angel will be executed in the morning. I expect you to be there."

Gideon jerked another nod.

"You can leave now."

THAT NIGHT GIDEON didn't sleep. He sat on the window seat in his bedroom and looked out over the island. A hard rain fell against the window pane so all he could see was a soft watery reflection of his own tormented face. Was he a bad man who had enticed an innocent girl to her doom? Was he an innocent man who had been enticed by a bad girl? Was there any way to save her? Did he want to save her? Whom had he failed? He couldn't control the images that played through his head at random—his father's disappointed face, his grandmother's disappointed face, Angel's laughing eyes, his brother lying ill, Angel's lowered eyes hiding disappointment. On and on, his memories fought for screen time as his mind reeled. If he hadn't been so reckless, none of this would have happened.

In the morning, he watched as a crowd gathered at the Golden Bowl. He watched as thirty-four male members of the Seven were executed. Each person was executed by a bullet through the head. A board had been put up to catch the backsplash. The bodies were removed almost as quickly as they fell. Still, the air stank of death as red blood and brain matter sprayed through the air, only to fall onto ground already saturated from the rain the night before.

Angel was the only female member and the only one from the island. She was to be the last execution. Gideon felt his hands tremble and then his body as he waited for Angel to be brought out.

The raucous crowd grew quiet as well. Angel was very social, and lots of the island's citizens had interacted with her in some way. Some in the crowd cried silently for her. It was extremely rare for the king to order the execution of an islander. Gideon braced himself for Angel's name to be called. It was customary for the secretary to the royal executioner to read out the name of the prisoner about to be executed.

"Former Minister John Kang," the secretary's booming voice called out over the public speakers.

Gideon's eyes widened in shock, and his gaze sought his father's. His father was standing beside him and continued to look straight ahead as he said, "While he is entirely innocent of his daughter's crime, he has decided to take her punishment."

"Angel?" Gideon croaked out.

"Life imprisonment," his father replied.

They watched together as the executioner shot Minister Kang and his body fell. The entire crowd was openly crying.

"An innocent man lost his life today," his father said as he nodded to the royal executioner and walked away.

Gideon followed, feeling lost and unanchored.

As their security detail escorted them to the car, they walked past the prison staff loading Angel back into the van that had come with thirty-five prisoners and would return with only one. Tears and grief marred her normally beautiful laughing face.

For an instant, Gideon's gaze met hers. Her expression of disbelief mirrored his own.

Gideon finally tore his gaze away and walked on resolutely. In the car, he and his father sat silent and alone. His father had requested that no guards sit in the car with them. As they pulled up to The Red Palace, his father finally spoke.

"I never thought I would ever be as displeased with you as I am today. Minister Kang's death weighs heavy on my heart. Your brother's situation is breaking my heart. And yet, you've suffered nothing." His father closed his eyes tight and took a deep breath before continuing. "I am holding my anger back by only the thinnest of threads. Go to the temple and stay until I call you back. The car will take you."

Gideon nodded his acquiescence. "Mom? Gabe? Ya Ya?" He was asking what his father would tell them. The news of the executions would be rampant.

His father exited the car without answering.

5
EDEN, ADJUSTMENT

$\mathcal{M}$y first day of classes, I got up at the set time to make my bed, neaten my room, and head to the communal washroom. Kaitlyn and Bethany had warned me the night before that the water would be lukewarm at best, if not downright cold. Each class used the washroom in fifteen-minute increments with the fourth-years going first and the first-years last, so it was no surprise that there was no hot water by the time the first-years came in.

The washroom was huge with two wide entrances, one leading to a long row of toilet stalls and sinks, and the other leading to a long row of shower stalls with outside hooks for towels and robes. On the wall opposite the two entrances were stacks of fluffy white towels and robes below a series of opaque windows.

The washroom was quieter than I imagined it would be. Perhaps the silence was due to the presence of two older ladies, one at each end of the opaque windows. Their hair was an impossible mass of short monochromatic black curls against deeply lined and grooved pale faces dotted with age spots. Both had slight stoops to their backs. Their dark black eyes were like the lens of a camera, seeing everything and revealing nothing. Everyone seemed aware of them, but no one spoke to them, only giving them the slightest of nods in passing.

Despite the cold water, the washroom itself seemed to have good heating. When I looked in one of the mirrors, I couldn't clearly see my face. The invisible heat had combined with the humidity from the water and the fragrance from the soaps to make a visible layer of fragrant condensation on the mirrors.

Kaitlyn and Bethany had told me there was an optional "beauty room" right next to the washroom where girls blow-dried and styled their hair and painted their faces. Apparently, according to Kaitlyn, there was a specialized program that used scientific data to recommend colors and products after using a scanner to view your skin tone and texture, hair color and length, and facial feature dimensions. I wasn't sure I trusted Kaitlyn's scientific explanation, but I had a more practicable reason for avoiding the beauty room. My hair was a minimum two-hour job and one usually reserved for the weekend. The idea of putting makeup on was too intimating to try on my first day of school. I had only been allowed to wear light-colored lip gloss back home and then only on special occasions.

Classes started at 8:45 a.m. On my first day of class, I had Spanish and French in the morning. A Mrs. Berger taught both languages. She was a petite, wiry woman who wore her hair pulled back into a tight bun with one lone curl escaping in the front. The silvery threads in her shining black hair matched her silvery dangling earrings. In time, I would come to realize that Mrs. Berger always wore black. On my first day of her class, she wore a beautiful blouse of black lace with a brocaded black skirt and black pumps.

My French and Spanish classes were each ninety minutes long with a fifteen-minute break in between. There were the same seven first-year girls in both classes, including Kaitlyn and Bethany. While the classes were conducted entirely in their respective languages, I found them to be very basic. My mother had made me do entire days of speaking in either French or Spanish from age six so that I could speak both languages fluently.

While the language part was not difficult, I didn't know what to make of Mrs. Berger. Her face was hard to read, except when she was displeased. Kaitlyn got a turn of phrase wrong, and Mrs. Berger frowned her disapproval and told her to study harder. When Mrs. Berger turned to write something on the whiteboard, Kaitlyn stuck out her tongue. Bethany smiled and looked down at her electronic notepad, continually typing. I was sitting between them and wasn't sure what to make of their little rebellion, so I kept my eyes lowered and kept typing like Bethany.

After morning classes, I was more than ready for a longer break and lunch. Mrs. Berger, however, told me to remain after class. Without preamble, she told me I didn't belong in her class and that she would speak with Mrs. Grey about moving me to higher level foreign language classes. I should expect my schedule to change. She sat down at her desk, indicating that the conversation was over before I had barely mumbled my thanks.

After lunch, Bethany and Kaitlyn invited me to go for a walk. I was happy they asked, because I was unsure what to do with myself. My next class was more than an hour away at 2 p.m. I was also curious about where we could go. As we started the walk, Kaitlyn was full of conversation.

"Why was Mrs. Stout moved to another house?" Kaitlyn asked. "Moving from our house to the Jasmine House? That's a big demotion."

"I don't know why you try to make sense of everything," Bethany replied. "Nothing here makes sense. Why would someone pay two hundred thousand dollars for each one of us?"

I felt like an idiot. No, I was an idiot. I hadn't even questioned Mrs. Grey's statement about the money. There was no reason for anyone to pay such money! The world was full of nice, beautiful girls.

"Maybe we're especially beautiful?" Kaitlyn asked. Both Bethany and I stopped walking and looked at her with our mouths open in shock.

"Well, you have to admit that the girls at the Jade Vine House are better-looking than average," Kaitlyn persisted.

"No, we're not better-looking than average. We just know how to make ourselves look that way. Can we walk, please? This conversation is getting stupider by the minute!" Bethany said before stalking away.

Kaitlyn and I stared at Bethany's retreating back before following her on the path. Kaitlyn's cheeks were bright red. While I was starting to think that Kaitlyn wasn't the brightest star, I felt bad for her after Bethany's insult. In Kaitlyn's defense, I'd noticed there was an awful lot of emphasis on beauty at the Joseph Hyde School for Exceptional Girls.

Back home, the emphasis at church and at home was always on inner beauty and presenting yourself in a clean and modest way. Makeup was expected to be discreet and generally discouraged unless you were about to be married or were married. Clothing was expected to cover everything from the neck to just below the knee.

Women generally adhered to expectations, except there was a lot of leeway in how they covered themselves. Many women wore clothing that emphasized an hourglass figure. Government scientists had determined a certain waist-to-hip ratio as ideal for childbearing, so women wanted to emphasize the "ideal" waist, even if half of them would end up using a licensed surrogate.

Back home, discussions about makeup and clothes had generally seemed above my age range, and while I wanted to generally look presentable, I was not in any great rush to be considered an adult. I wanted to remain home with my parents for as long as possible. When I got my period, I cried. Mary was supposedly around fourteen years of age when she had Baby Jesus, but I was not yet ready for babies, celestial or otherwise.

I didn't have a good feeling about someone paying money for me. It gave me a sense of obligation and not in a good way, more in a panic-inducing way. I resolved to shelve my uneasiness for the moment and focus on getting to know Bethany and Kaitlyn.

We continued beyond the campus green and on past the east building, moving along paths and trails that were not visible from my room window. I was surprised we had the freedom to go such a distance, but I supposed we really didn't have the means to travel anywhere else. Walking relaxed me. Eventually, I moved to the front with Kaitlyn and Bethany behind me. I felt looser the farther we walked, as though everything inside me was not so chained and controlled.

I was almost fully seduced by the birds' chirping, the sun shining, the grass waving, and the silent companionship, when I saw the wrought iron fence with barbed wire at the top and electrical wires running perpendicular to the iron posts. Just inside the fence, I could see an all-terrain mud-splattered dark-green jeep with two men leaning on the side, rifles held loosely in their hands. "Giovanni" and another man of about the same size and age both had on blazing white tanks, and their muscular arms were covered with tattoos. I remembered from my window gazing that the outer edges of the campus were surrounded by tall trees bearing heavy green foliage. I hadn't realized the trees shielded this restraining fence.

Bethany touched my arm lightly and put her finger to her mouth, indicating that we should be quiet. We were hidden from the view of the guards, and the three of us quietly backtracked without talking.

When we were close to the Jade Vine House, Kaitlyn said, "Why were Giovanni and that other guy there? There are cameras everywhere, and the gate is sensitive to human touch. There's no need for guards."

"They were hoping to catch a girl from one of the other houses walking alone," Bethany replied, her voice grim.

"You mean, if one of us walked alone, nothing would happen?" I asked.

"We're untouchable by the guards. They can only restrain us if we try to escape," Bethany replied. "We're only touchable once we leave here." She gave a quick, mirthless laugh.

"But how do they know who belongs to which house?" I asked.

"The logo on your uniform has a microchip with your info. They can read the chip with their phones," Bethany replied. "They can use the logo to track us, too."

"But the logo is on everything, even my . . . underthings?" I inquired.

"Exactly!" Bethany replied, rolling her eyes at the insanity of it.

I guessed the microchip explained our ability to wander the campus. "But do the girls from the other houses wander outside? I thought we're not supposed to interact?" I asked.

"I'm not sure where they can go," Bethany said, frowning.

"Then how do you know the guards catch the other girls?" Kaitlyn asked as she stopped walking.

Bethany and I stopped as well, but there was no answer from

Bethany. She just looked at the ground, moving her feet back and forth and hugging herself.

"See, you don't know everything," Kaitlyn said as she rolled her eyes away from Bethany and resumed walking.

"I saw it," Bethany said.

"You saw what? . . . Oh!" Kaitlyn said, her eyes widening as she stopped again.

"I feel bad for those girls," Bethany said with a sigh as her shoulders slumped.

"Me too," I said.

"Me three," Kaitlyn said with her arms wide.

We all hugged, but feelings of guilt nagged at me. I knew I hadn't caused the other girls' situation, but I felt guilt nonetheless.

"We just have to pray on it," I said, something I had heard my mom say often enough.

Bethany and Kaitlyn nodded, and we rushed back to be on time for our next class.

I found Household Budgeting to be more interesting than I thought it would be. The course was about how to turn savings from spending money and gifts like jewels into wealth in your own name. Looking at the course syllabus, we would be learning about stocks, bonds, and interest rates. We were each assigned an imaginary household budget, and each week our assignment was to pretend-buy household items and figure out where to put the money saved. In your fourth year, the school matched "real" money with the amount of "pretend" money you saved or grew in value over the course of the four years. The real money match was considered your graduation gift.

I was not good at math. My mother would get very frustrated trying to teach it to me. She would get an edge to her voice that said she was out of patience but trying to pretend otherwise. I would start whining a little. Sometimes, on not very good days, the lessons would end with my mother sending me to my room where I would throw myself across my bed, sobbing while she drank tea and played worship music loud enough to drown out my sobs. When my dad came home, he would do the same lessons with me, but for some reason, I learned much more easily from him. He was able to break down concepts into small, manageable bits.

I found that the thought of having my own money when I graduated was a powerful motivator. Hopefully, my husband would allow me to keep an account in my own name once we were married. I wondered what I would do if my spouse was horrid to the point that I could not endure. With no money, what could I do? My mother seemed to control the money in our household, but my father hated sitting down and paying bills. My friend Eliza's mom had to get permission from her husband for each expenditure. I would've preferred to be in my mom's situation.

In any case, I liked the teacher, a seventyish-looking woman of Asian descent with totally white hair worn in a bun held back with two intricately designed silver hairpins. She exuded confidence and goodwill. I was surprised to learn later that she was one of the few teachers who wasn't faculty and didn't live at the school. Bethany told me the school was bequeathed a ton of money ten years before, and one of the requirements to receive the money was that an outside teacher be brought in to teach every student money management. Kaitlyn added that sometimes teachers joined the classes as students as well.

I thought English and History would be my favorite classes. I loved reading and discussing books, and I've always been fascinated by how ordinary people lived many years ago. I soon learned, though, that we were not allowed to read books that mentioned other religions, contained any kissing or touching, had characters in non-traditional gender roles, and/or contained swear words. I understood that the goal was to keep our minds pure, not defiled by false doctrines, but I was still bored by these classes.

It was not like my parents didn't place restrictions on what I read, but the school seemed to take rules to the extreme. My mom hated books with poor grammar, run-on sentences, and glaring typos or misspellings. I was not allowed to read such books, no matter what the topic. She said she did not want me to have any inkling that such sloppiness was acceptable.

As for the books I could read, no topics were off limits if the content was not too explicit and if unchristian values were not portrayed as the right values. My mom was especially fond of assigning books with redemption as a primary theme. We would discuss the fictitious characters, sometimes for hours, as if they were real people. My father would sometimes interrupt our discussions to "bring us back into the real world." All the books we read were available at the Sunny City's lending library, which only carried books approved by the Home Inspectors.

Here, at the Joseph Hyde School for Exceptional Girls, the reading material was much more limited. Any character wrestling with questions of theology automatically made a book "unacceptable" as a book about "other religions," a groom kissing his new bride was deemed "sexually explicit," and a book with a teenage girl working in her family's general goods store was pulled from the electronic library of books we could access because of her non-traditional gender role.

After reading my first assigned reading, I felt like I had eaten cotton candy. The words were sweet and fluffy, but there was no substance to them. I found myself hungering to read a book that would take me out of myself and take me to another world where my heart and mind would get caught up in another's struggles and joys. Reality seemed more palatable when there were moments of escape. To say I was bitterly disappointed by the lack of reading choices would be an understatement. I was ashamed when I remembered how I needled my parents about censoring my reading choices, not realizing how much liberty they had provided me. Here, I couldn't even write the stories I wanted to write and create my own fiction because that was censored as well.

As for History, we only learned about our country's independence from England and the history of our country after the Savior's Revolution. Everything in between was a downward spiral into immoral behavior and so deemed not fitting for our youthful ears.

I kept silent about the many hours my father and I had spent reading aloud from his old history books. With him, I had learned about the Native Americans originally in the country, the world wars, the civil wars, and the conflicts in some parts of the world that seemed older than time and yet never ended. I learned that over fragrant jasmine tea at a world leaders' summit, representatives of America's Saviors and representatives from Country X came to a mutually agreeable proposition. America's Saviors promised Country X's prime minister that he could increase the interest rates on the money the American government had borrowed from it. All Country X had to do to earn the fiscal bounty was lend enough soldiers to help rural militia groups fight the battle for true American values.

With the help of those loaned foreign soldiers, rural militia groups won the civil war that followed the summit. A constitutional convention was belatedly called. The First Amendment to the U.S. Constitution was repealed, and Christianity was established as the national religion while other religions were explicitly banned. The government took complete control of all forms of media. Anyone who did not have the means to escape to other countries and who refused to profess Christianity as his or her personal religion was immediately executed. I cringed when I read about the executions. I was a Christian, but I thought right living was a better way to convert others than fear.

Still, my father's history books seemed like fantastical stories, never quite real. He kept the books on an old memory stick that he hid in an earth-colored vase sprouting pastel flowers. He figured Chief Inspector Brown would never look in the vase, and he was right.

I overheard my parents arguing once about the books. I had gotten up to get a glass of water but stopped when I heard my mother's voice. She was speaking quietly, but I could hear the tinge of annoyed anger in her voice.

"Stephen, you are putting us in danger by teaching her history. She's not supposed to know all that stuff."

I didn't hear anything else for a long moment, and just when I was about to creep silently back to my room, I heard my father say, "I can't not teach her history. If she doesn't know it, how can she be prepared for whatever comes next?"

"Yes," my mom replied. "I get it. But what if she inadvertently says something she shouldn't? It would be a disaster for all of us, and she would believe she caused the disaster."

My father continued the lessons, but he made me promise again not to mention them outside our home. I never slipped up and said something inadvertent in Sunny City, but I was homeschooled. There wasn't much opportunity to slip up. At my new school, I was so afraid I would slip up in History class and reveal something I wasn't supposed to know that I would frequently have tension headaches during the class.

To make matters worse, the Art of Conversation, which I thought would be a moderately easy class, proved to be excruciating. We had to practice having conversations about the weather: "Nice weather we're having this fall;" clothes: "That color really compliments you;" and gardens: "Those flowers are still fragrant."

Find-A-Compliment exercises were the most difficult. Those were conversations where you listened mostly but prompted the other person to continue chatting by complimenting them about something they just disclosed. If you couldn't think of anything complimentary, you just gave one-word enthusiastic responses like, "Wonderful!"

Kaitlyn, I discovered, was a natural in this class. She chatted on about virtually nothing with such grace, poise, and charm that you only realized afterward that she said nothing of importance. I looked at her with envy several times during the two-hour class when I found myself sitting next to my assigned partner in embarrassing silence, realizing I had once again answered a question with just a "yes" or "no," leaving little room for the conversation to continue to flow.

Unlike Mrs. Berger, Mrs. Post let her expressions really show, and by the end of the first class, I had been reprimanded so many times I lost count: "Remember, Eden, to engage your partner. No one likes to chat with a log. Find a compliment." Remembering that poor performance was not really an option, I resolved to do better.

At least Domestic Arts wasn't too bad. Before the first class, Kaitlyn and Bethany put me at ease.

"This is the easiest class ever," Kaitlyn said cheerfully. "Just easy-peasy assignments on running a house and making it beautiful. There are even a few lessons thrown in on managing household staff."

If I was to be home as a wife, I wasn't sure why I would need a staff to do basic things I could do myself, but I was too embarrassed to question it.

Kaitlyn looped one arm around Bethany and one around me, and we walked three abreast as she dragged us along to class. We all had to go to the class but I—and I suspected Bethany—would have preferred a more sedate pace.

"This is also the most boring class ever," Bethany said.

"Is that why you take a nap every class?" Kaitlyn asked.

Bethany stuck out her tongue at Kaitlyn, who returned the favor.

"Now, girls, is that any way for ladies to behave?" Mrs. Flint said.

My mouth fell open. I hadn't even seen Mrs. Flint approach.

"No, Mrs. Flint," Bethany and Kaitlyn said together. Mrs. Flint looked at me with one eyebrow raised.

"No, Mrs. Flint," I stammered out.

When Mrs. Flint moved on, Bethany whispered to me, "Nice, real nice."

My face flushed red as we entered the large classroom.

At least Bethany and Kaitlyn's words proved true. The teacher, a Mrs. Askew, spent fifteen minutes at the beginning of the class explaining the lesson on ironing corduroy fabrics and then allowed us the rest of the two-hour class period to apply the lesson. Each girl had one corduroy piece of fabric to iron.

"Yawn, what do I do next?" Bethany asked as she finished up her piece of fabric. She didn't seem to be talking to anyone, and no one answered her.

I finished my assignment and waited to see if the teacher would come by to check. I thought she was reading a book at her desk, but on closer inspection, I could see that her eyes were closed. Shocked, I looked around at the other girls. Some took naps, like Bethany, but others were working on their own projects. I saw Kaitlyn pull out a beautiful peach-colored fabric with embroidered white flowers.

When she saw me looking at the fabric, she said, "I'm making a skirt to go with the white blouse I plan to make later."

"But there's no place to wear it," I said, half statement, half question.

"The Saturday night dinners," she said as though this explained everything.

"Huh?" I asked.

"You get to wear non-uniform clothes at dinner on Saturdays," said another girl as she doodled on a piece of paper. "Supposedly, you can borrow something from the dress closet, but the third- and fourth-years take everything good."

"I prefer making my own anyway," said Kaitlyn.

"I don't," Bethany said sleepily, stretching herself awake. "Please tell me this class is over."

As Christmas approached, I gradually found a rhythm to my days. I could keep up with the work, and I liked my friendships with Kaitlyn and Bethany. I had the sensation, though, of marking time, of counting down the days until I could really live. I pushed to the back of my mind the disturbing questions of why someone would pay to marry us and what would happen once we graduated. Would I really be reunited with my family?

One night, a few weeks before Christmas, I was getting ready to turn in, when I heard a scream. It sounded as if it came from outside. I ran to the window to look out, but just when I got to the window, I stopped, remembering Bethany's words. I didn't want to see Giovanni or the other man with one of the girls from the other houses.

"It's an owl," I told myself as I closed the window with my eyes shut tight. I quickly lay down, and with one side of my head pressed into the bed, I pressed a pillow on the other side. I had the errant thought that maybe I should pull the pillow over my face and end it all. I was so shocked at my thought that I got up and paced the small confines of my room. I went from my door to almost to the window and back again, just to start the cycle all over again. Fatigue plagued me, but I felt compelled to move. When morning's first rays of sunlight came softly into my room, I sat on the floor and cried.

The day before Christmas was a free day, no classes. The other girls decided to go for walks, make snowmen, sing carols, and finish their Christmas Eve dinner outfits. I decided to sleep in. My mom used to say that the joy of Christmas made it a hard holiday for some others. I had nodded my head sympathetically but didn't really understand her meaning. I would never be in the "other" group. I guess that was why my mom used to say, "Never say never."

In any case, I didn't get out of bed until after noon. I began my late day with prayers more earnest than they had been over the past few months. I prayed for my parents, that they were safe and well and not bothered by Inspector Brown. I prayed the usual prayers for the earth and her leaders. I also prayed for my new friends, Bethany and Kaitlyn. Their friendship was special to me.

I had been friends with Mary and Eliza back home, but they were friendships that developed because our parents were friends. Our parents went to the same local church, lived in the same community, and by wordless agreement decreed that their similarly aged children should be friends too. That's not to say we didn't have plenty of fun together, playing make-believe and having silly conversations. But Bethany and Kaitlyn were special because *they* chose me, not their parents. We were advised not to talk too much about our individual family circumstances, but I guessed that Kaitlyn was raised in a happier home than Bethany. After praying, I felt more peaceful than I had in a long time. The sadness from being apart from my family was still with me, but for the first time, I had confidence that the sadness was a burden I could carry.

Looking out the window, I took pleasure at the sight of fluffy snow everywhere. There was laughter as girls celebrated their day of freedom and played in the snow. The whole scene reminded me of those winter snow globes my dad would buy me on his way home from various business trips. I had at least a dozen of those things in my room back home. Looking in the snow globe, no one would notice that the Jade Vine House girls only interacted with girls from their own house. That was the beauty of beauty. It distracted from the ugliness of life.

Finally, I turned away to get ready for dinner, making a small sigh of pleasure at the red plaid sheath dress hanging off a hook on my wall. It was the first dress I'd made myself, and without false modesty, I could say I'd done a halfway decent job. It was then that I heard the scream.

This screaming was not the sort that led you to ponder whether to get help or not. It practically pulled me by my arms and propelled me out the door without any conscious thought on my part. At the bottom of the stairs, a crowd had gathered around a girl who was on her knees crying and saying, "Please," over and over. Her voice was desperate.

I went over to join the crowd, but there was no room to get a good look at what was going on. I stood next to the school nurse and behind Mrs. Flint, who stood with the washroom ladies, one on each side of her. Her hands were clenched. I overheard one of the washroom ladies murmur that the girl had been switched with her sister, the girl who was supposed to come. The other washroom lady shook her head as if against the folly of such an idea.

I heard hard steps behind me and turned to see Giovanni and the man I had seen him with before striding toward the crowd. The other girls saw too and shrank away in remembered fear, giving the girl on her knees a direct view of them. I didn't recognize her. I knew I should do something to stop what I feared was about to happen, but I did nothing but shrink back with the other girls. I looked at Mrs. Flint and saw that her face was closed, the tenseness in her body the only indication that she was not pleased.

I looked from the cruel anticipation on Giovanni's face to the girl's face and stared in surprise. She was now mysteriously smiling, her face still red and wet from crying. The day's last remaining rays of sunlight came through a window and backlit her long mass of thick, wavy dark hair, making her look like a girl from a long-ago painting. I saw her raise her hand to her lips and heard Mrs. Flint gasp and step forward, only to be stopped by the school nurse who had stepped forward as well. But in the nurse's case, it was to reach out with one muscular arm and hold Mrs. Flint back.

"All of you step away from the girl, now," the nurse said with such authority that all of us girls obeyed.

Giovanni ignored the nurse as he knelt and grabbed the girl's face roughly with his right hand, his thumb and fingers pressing hard into her round cheeks. To everyone's surprise, she grabbed both of his arms with her hands and kissed him firmly. We collectively gasped in shock and then stood with our mouths silently open as a frothy, bloody white mess came out of her mouth and her ears, and her whole body went slack. From the stench, it seemed her bowels had opened too.

I felt nausea rising in me as Giovanni jumped back in horror, wiping his mouth with his forearm. He turned away from the girl and toward the nurse. The look on his face was murderous.

"What did she do to me?" he growled.

"Don't move, and I'll do what I can to help you," the nurse replied. "Eden, hurry and go and get the square metal case on the top shelf in my office. It's painted red with a white square on it. Go now!"

I moved toward her office. When I was almost there, I heard screaming and footsteps. Turning, I saw Giovanni's partner running away, his eyes wide with fright. I hurried to get the square metal case and ran back to the crowd. I couldn't have been gone more than two or three minutes.

Back with the crowd, I saw that Giovanni's body had slumped to the floor and gone through the same purging as had the unknown girl. The stench his body released was even more nauseating. I held out the metal case weakly to the nurse, who took it, but she looked very worried.

My stomach rolled, but I couldn't see any nearby trash cans. I turned to run to one of the small washrooms on the first floor, realized I wouldn't make it, and ended up vomiting in a tall potted plant just a few steps away. I was a little embarrassed but heard other sounds of vomiting and was perversely relieved that I wasn't the only one.

"Mrs. Flint, we need to contact the CDC," the nurse said in a low voice. "I'm almost positive that girl had some sort of biological agent she swallowed; it was not just poison. I think it's RZ932, which only acts once it enters the body. If the girls don't touch the liquid from the girl or Giovanni, I think they should be fine. I'm not sure, though. There's nothing anyone can do for RZ932 exposure."

My stomach sank at the idea of going through what I just saw. I was about to move toward Kaitlyn and Bethany, but then I heard Mrs. Flint speak quietly.

"I can't take a chance on this news leaking. We have plenty of neutralizing agents; put something down. The girls can get cleaned up, and we'll all be in self-quarantine."

The nurse just stared at Mrs. Flint for a moment. "My job is to ensure the health and safety of each of these girls. Is it not almost immoral to worry about publicity at a time like this?"

Mrs. Flint replied tartly, "What do you think will happen to the girls if this news gets out? Why do you think the girl had the biological agent, anyway? She didn't pick it up at the corner store."

I looked around and saw that all the girls had moved back from the bodies on the floor. Everyone's faces looked drawn and tired. No one had the strength for good posture, either leaning against the walls or slouching in chairs. The stench and presence of the dead bodies were like a paralyzing tableau, made even more unpalatable by the scent of fear and vomit.

The sun had run away for the night, and shadows loomed, relieved only by a few scented candles that had been lit. Into this dreaded silence, the bells rang for the five o'clock Christmas service, making everyone start in surprise, but no one spoke or moved.

After a prolonged silence, the nurse spoke. "Girls, it looks as though these two came down with food poisoning that was life-threatening. We are going to self-quarantine, just to make sure the situation doesn't spread through the school."

I was a little startled by her explanation. I had just heard her saying it was RZ something, which did not sound like food poisoning. I realized that she couldn't see me.

Bethany asked, "What was it that gave them food poisoning?" There was a hint of skepticism in her voice.

"The fruitcake," replied the nurse.

Another girl named Maria asked, "What will happen to their bodies?" She waved a hand in the general direction of the deceased.

"They will be cremated. Also, I may as well tell you now that Giovanni's partner will no longer be working for the school. The school had already made the decision to move him before today. Now, I need you all to cooperate. I will need to put down some neutralizing agents before I have the crematory come to get the bodies. I will spray you girls as well with a spray-form neutralizing agent before you leave this room. Avoid touching your mouth, eyes, or any open cuts or sores. You girls will need to do quiet activities in your room for the next day or so."

The other girls all nodded to indicate their acquiescence.

"Where is Eden?" said Mrs. Flint.

Kaitlyn saved me by saying, "She went to the washroom. Here she is, coming back now." She waved her hand to indicate that I should keep walking toward them, obscuring the fact that I hadn't, in fact, been walking.

I joined her and Bethany. I kept my eyes down because I was afraid they would betray me. However, surprising myself, I asked, "What was the girl's name?"

Mrs. Flint responded, "We think her name was Rosemary. We expected her sister Ginger to arrive, but it looks like Rosemary arrived instead."

I felt a small measure of satisfaction that we at least had a tentative name. Somehow, the thought that the girl, Rosemary, would die nameless and unrecognized seemed even more terrible.

We survived the quarantine and had a much quieter Christmas celebration a week later. While I was immensely relieved that neither I nor anyone else came down with "food poisoning," I felt miserable. I had the feeling of saying expected lines in a play. I wanted to cry and weep at the madness of it all, but I could see that Mrs. Flint was watching us all closely. It seemed to me that she watched me more than the others. What would happen if one of us cracked?

I began to daydream a lot, surprising myself with the complexity and emotion in my alternative universes. Scrubbed and censored books gave me no pleasure. I often spent those precious minutes before sleep daydreaming in worlds of my own creation. Sometimes, I even resented sleep for taking me out of my dream world, especially when I daydreamed about Rosemary. In my daydreams, I was not quietly watching her die but finding improbable ways to keep her alive.

But one night, Rosemary refused to follow the script I had set. Despite my best efforts, I slipped from daydreaming into sleep, where a dream stepped in without invitation. In this dream, I awoke to the sound of screaming and the smell of smoke. In the way of dreams, I knew I had to find Rosemary. The scene shifted, and Rosemary and I ran hand in hand toward open gates. The heat was almost unbearable. I was nearly suffocating on the fumes, and my face dripped with sweat. I didn't stop running because we were so close to the gate. But then, Rosemary let go of my hand. I turned to grab her, but she just gave me the same mysterious smile she had just before she died.

"Come on!" I choked out. "We're almost there!"

She just shook her head as she smiled and said, "The past cannot be undone. Don't fail to see the open gates." Then she disappeared into the ground.

I heard a sound and turned. The gates were closing! I ran toward the closing gates, and that was when I woke up, choking on saliva that seemed to have gone down the wrong way.

My sheets were so wet that I smelled them to make certain the wetness was from sweat and not urine. Still caught in the dream, I ran to the window to make sure there was no fire. With my head leaning against the cool window, I prayed not to dream such dreams anymore. I wanted lucid dreams directed by me. For without such dreams, how would I survive the long hours of the day?

6

GIDEON, A PRICE TO BE PAID

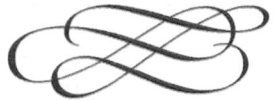

*O*n the long drive to the temple, Gideon could not own his mind, which, on a normal day, would flit happily from thought to thought like a little hummingbird. Today there was no place his mind felt welcome. What should he think about that would bring him peace? Anger was even lost to him, for against whom could he vent his anger? It was his own actions that caused this tragic turn of events.

Gideon closed his eyes and tried to make his mind blank, but it ignored his will and just kept replaying the day's horrors. He turned this way and that way, but there was no way for him to run from his own self, no matter how roomy the seats behind the driver were. There was room for at least six, with two rows of three seats that faced each other over a small console doubling as a table.

In desperation, Gideon remembered that some of the cars in the royal fleet included bottles of expensive wines or other spirits to give as gifts in case such an occasion arose. With shaking fingers, he checked the console, and to his relief, he found four bottles of baijiu, each wrapped in a luxurious purple and gold velvet. He unwrapped a bottle and drank, thankful for the tinted windows, but still the tears flowed, his hands shook, and he wanted to jump out of his body and run. So, he drank the entire bottle and lost consciousness, his mind at last taking a break from the war within.

When the driver pulled up at the temple, Prince Gideon was unresponsive, his face flushed. Several of the temple's good brothers carried the spare heir out of the vehicle and into the temple's infirmary, where he was treated for alcohol poisoning. Three days later, Gideon opened his eyes, the cobwebs of dream and alcohol fading from his mind as he looked around.

He was taking up the third bed out of a row of about a dozen medical beds, the heads of which were shoved against the stainless steel medical walls that held everything an infirmary could need, including robotic arms to dispense medication. The first two beds were occupied by elderly men, probably temple brothers if their shaved heads were anything to go by. Another man with a shaved head but with a white medical jacket sat at one of the two desks opposite the beds, concentrating on the electronic notepad in his hand. At the other desk sat Luke and James, looking straight at him. Gideon found, to his further shame, that he could not meet their gaze. He shuttered his eyes and pretended to be falling back asleep. Would his life forever be this gray hell of bitter regret?

"You're awake," said a voice Gideon recognized.

Incredulous, he turned his head to look at the speaker. It was Luke. Luke and James both stood at the left side of his bed.

Gideon sat up, groaning and making a big show of rubbing his eyes. "What are the two of you doing here?"

Luke and James shared a look before Luke spoke again. "We are your personal guards. Where else would we be?"

Gideon felt a surprising burst of gratitude that his father still cared to send the guards, but he wasn't sure why both would be with him. "Shouldn't one of you be with Gabe?"

"Your brother is the one that sent us here," James said, his tone carefully flat.

Gideon looked more closely at him and noticed how tired he looked, the lines around his eyes deeper than usual. With surprise, Gideon noticed the gray silently creeping into James's hair at the temple.

Looking sideways to Luke, Gideon could see his eyes were bleary from lack of sleep.

Even more surprising, the guards weren't dressed exactly alike as they usually were. Their daily uniform was a well-cut black suit, tailored white shirt, black tie, dark shades, and professionally shined black shoes. Today, Luke's tie was missing, and the top button of his shirt was unbuttoned, while James kept his tie but left his jacket. Both had more stubble on their cheeks than Gideon had seen before.

Steeling himself, he asked, "What has happened?"

Again, Luke and James shared a look but remained silent.

Irritated, Gideon sat up straighter. "Tell me. That's a direct order."

Luke and James looked at him as though he had grown two heads. "We don't take orders from you," they said in unison.

Gideon sighed. "Ugh, back to this again. I know you take orders directly from the king, blah, blah, blah, and blah. I've heard it a million times."

"You've heard it a million times because it never sinks in," said Luke.

"So why are you here on Gabe's order if you only take orders from the king?" Gideon asked.

Both Luke and James flushed red and avoided looking at him before James finally said, "We've been suspended."

"What!" Gideon said, shocked. His father's trust in Luke and James had been unwavering. What changed?

"Was it because . . ." Gideon stopped, unsure of how much the guards knew.

"Yes, it was because of that," Luke said, his voice not quite managing the same level of neutrality that James had achieved earlier.

Gideon felt even more shame. His disgrace was their disgrace as well, for they had failed to inform the king of all of Gideon's social activities. Gideon was never explicit about his relationship with Angel, but it wouldn't have been difficult for the guards to figure out why Angel spent significantly more time than was necessary in the Merman Hotel's Royal Suite. When Angel would arrive at the suite, Luke, the guard normally assigned to Gideon, would frequently go and stand outside to "stretch his legs."

Beneath the thin infirmary sheet covering his lower body, Gideon's hands clenched the bedding beneath him as he took a breath and said, "I'm sorry."

James waved off the apology, shaking his head. "No need. We were negligent in our duties."

"*We* weren't exactly negligent," Luke said. "It seems someone forgot the rule that one should be careful about accepting food and drink."

"Luke!" James whisper-shouted in a stunned tone.

Gideon was shocked too. Luke and James enjoyed being the enforcers of the king's orders with respect to the princes, but they never took that authority too far.

"How did the first king die? His 'lady of the evening' poisoned him through a bottle of red wine she gave as a 'gift,'" Luke continued on, unrepentant. "But Romeo over here just had to—"

"Enough!" Gideon interrupted as anger, shame, and guilt spiked through him.

"Shhh . . ." said a querulous voice from the patient on the right of Gideon.

James said, "Sorry, sir," before turning his attention back to Gideon. "We don't want to distress you. We know the punishment could have been worse." They all knew the punishment could have been immediate dismissal and permanent disgrace, so James was correct, but Gideon didn't like being the cause of their current suspension.

"If you're suspended, why are you here again," he asked.

"Actually, your father did fire us," James began.

"What!" Gideon exclaimed. "I thought you said you were just suspended."

"This is an infirmary, not an arena. Shhh!" The patient to Gideon's right sounded more irritated.

"My apologies," Gideon said as he nodded his head respectfully, thinking the other patient probably didn't know he was talking to a prince.

"Brother Li, I still need to finish my daily check for you." The man in the doctor's coat had turned toward them, speaking authoritatively. "Please wrap up your conversation in the next ten minutes."

Brother Li? Gideon thought to himself before he corrected the doctor. "Actually, it's Prince Li, and I'll need fifteen."

The doctor opened his mouth like he was going to say something, but then he nodded respectfully and turned back to his desk.

Gideon turned his attention back to the guards and noticed Luke was shaking his head at him. Gideon raised one of his eyebrows in silent inquiry.

"You never change—" Luke began but was cut off by James, who waved his hands as though shushing Luke.

"Getting back to the original topic, your father was rightfully angry with us and terminated our employment," James said.

"Told us never to show our faces in front of him again," Luke interjected.

"That too," James admitted. "Unfortunately, Gabriel came in right at that moment to ask what was going on—"

This time Gideon interrupted. "Then he doesn't know the situation?"

James shook his head to indicate no. "Your brother doesn't know the whole situation, and your father refused to tell him. I think he was afraid Gabriel was still too sick to be told bad news."

"But then Gabriel became just as angry as your father," Luke said. "He said if King Li—he used your father's official title—was going to fire us, he would just rehire us. Then—and you're not going to believe this— your father said he didn't fire us; he just suspended us."

Gideon didn't know what to say. "So that's why you're here?"

"Well, your brother said we were his employees for the duration of the suspension," James replied.

"Wh-What?" Gideon stammered in disbelief. His family was extremely civil to each other. They didn't act like characters in some sort of Korean drama.

"Your brother is worried about you being at the temple," James began. "He knows that there is something more at issue than . . ." James stopped and looked around before continuing, "Minister Kang's daughter."

"He is worried about me," Gideon said, realizing that a part of what had him unsettled was the physical separation from his brother. They rarely spent a day without conversing in person. Even with Gabriel's marriage, he still lived in The Red Palace.

"Yes, he is worried about you," Luke said, like it was hard to believe. "Do you know when your father will let you back?"

Gideon shook his head. Luke and James both seemed to go pale as their shoulders slumped in disappointment.

"Hey, hopefully, it won't be too bad," he said. "I heard they did away with the dungeons underground."

"You really are a piece of work, you—" Luke began in anger.

"Luke, take a walk," James said firmly.

Without a word, Luke turned and walked out of the infirmary.

James took a deep breath, bowed respectfully, and said, "Prince Gideon, my sincere apologies on Luke's behalf."

"Why is he so angry?" Gideon asked.

James hesitated, looking uncomfortable.

"Please tell me," Gideon pushed. He had never known Luke to behave so unprofessionally.

James sighed. "Prince, when one becomes a royal guard, one agrees to put another life before one's own in all respects. My time and allegiance belong to the royal family." Here, James hesitated again.

"Go on," Gideon encouraged.

"It's not quite proper for me to burden you, sir, with my own issues." James was clearly uncomfortable with their conversation.

"Do you want me to tell my brother and father that Luke should just be fired for behavior unbecoming a royal guard?" Gideon asked with one eyebrow raised. He saw the anger in James's eyes before he lowered his gaze.

"Luke's father-in-law, my uncle, is dying. The doctors say no more than six months," James said, his voice strained.

"I'm sorry," Gideon said, surprised that James and Luke were related by marriage.

James nodded, a wet sheen on his eyes. "Luke is also nervous about his wife. She is not handling her father's situation well. They are both hoping he can last long enough to meet his first grandchild."

"She's your cousin?" Gideon asked.

James nodded.

"And she's pregnant?" Gideon asked, surprised again at how little he knew about the guards.

"Four weeks to go," James said and held up his right hand to show his crossed fingers.

Gideon nodded before saying, "I understand he's under a lot of stress."

"Thank you for understanding, Prince," James said with a slight bow to his head.

"But, James," Gideon said. "With his family situation, shouldn't Luke be home with his family? Can't he request three days of family leave?"

James gave a wry smile. "Your brother was very clear, sir. We can't leave here—at all—until you do."

Gideon and James looked at each other, one gaze stricken and one gaze sad.

"YOU KNOW there are more efficient ways to kill yourself," the infirmary's physician stated. He had introduced himself as Dr. Jo.

"What?" Gideon responded, shocked.

"When you came in, your blood alcohol concentration was .35 percent."

"I drank that much?" Gideon asked, surprised.

"Yes, you did. Any higher, and we would have been hard-pressed to save you," Dr. Jo answered. "As it was, I had to arrange for the air medic to be on standby in case we needed to transport you to the hospital."

Gideon felt sucker punched by the information. Life was turning to quicksand around him. He managed to croak out, "Thank you, doctor."

"You can thank me by living right," Dr. Jo said sharply.

After Gideon's nod, he continued. "Did anyone explain the rules of the temple?"

"Brother Jo?" said the same querulous voice from earlier.

Dr. Jo immediately went to the other man's bedside. "Yes, Brother Adam?"

"You have plenty of work. If you don't mind, I can explain the rules to this young brother."

"Of course," replied Dr. Jo, bowing respectfully. He threw Gideon a contemptuous look before moving on to his desk.

Gideon tried to keep his face impassive as he absorbed anew the truth that he was a man worthy of condemnation. He turned to face Brother Adam, his mind in turmoil. He doubted he could retain anything Brother Adam had to say about the "rules."

"Your spirit is not at peace," said Brother Adam, his amber gaze on Gideon. There was no judgment in his tone, but Gideon thought he detected sadness. He pushed the thought away. How could this man who didn't even know him feel sadness for him?

"The last few days certainly could have gone better," Gideon said, not committing.

"How could they have gone better?" Brother Adam asked.

"Well, I wouldn't be in this infirmary for one," Gideon replied with a shrug of his shoulders.

"Another infirmary would have been better?" Brother Adam asked.

Gideon took a deep breath before responding. "This one is certainly not up to palace standards."

"But you aren't at the palace anymore."

"Do you know who I am?" Gideon asked.

"Do you know who you are?" Brother Adam replied.

Gideon shook his head in frustration, not up for a circular philosophical conversation. He replied brusquely, "It doesn't matter."

"Well, Mr. It Doesn't Matter, may I tell you a story?" Brother Adam asked.

Taking Gideon's silence as agreement, Brother Adam began, "Once upon a time—"

Gideon interrupted, "Are you seriously trying to tell me a fairy tale right now?" He turned on his side, facing away from Brother Adam, even more frustrated than before.

"Ah, but I promise you haven't heard this tale," Brother Adam said to

Gideon's back. He continued, unperturbed. "Once upon a time, in Crazy Horse Village, there lived a Lord Hamil who was the authority over the entire village. He lived in a monstrously large mansion seated high on a hill, far away from the villagers he ruled. He wasn't known as a fair and compassionate ruler, largely indifferent to the villagers. He wasn't faithful to his wife, and he wasn't pleased by his lack of sons. Instead, his wife had provided him with three daughters.

"For all his faults, though, Lord Hamil did have one genuine love. He loved his horses. If he wasn't eating or sleeping, Lord Hamil was out riding or training horses. He was competent at training horses as well, so much so that horses from his stable were much desired. Noble personages from far away would travel to his home to buy a Hamil race-horse. Even the king's stables were said to have one or two Hamil horses.

"Out of all his horses, though, Lord Hamil had a favorite. Her name was Queenie. She was an impressive height and a beautiful chestnut color. Most importantly, she was able to hold the lead in races against stallions. Lord Hamil loved her above all. He even gave large parties to celebrate her birthdays. He barely remembered, or cared to remember, his wife's birthday. Perhaps if he had, a terrible tragedy could have been diverted."

Gideon interrupted Brother Adam, turning to face him. "Let me guess the tragedy. The horse got a larger slice of cake than the wife?"

Brother Adam smiled but shook his head. "I'm not sure the horse liked cake, but that wasn't the tragedy. You see, Lady Hamil felt her husband put a horse before her in importance. She could abide other women but not a horse. She schemed to get rid of the horse. She found the least intelligent groom and with a bright smile handed him a special meal for Queenie, one laced with a plant root that would make the horse crazed. She hoped the horse would be wild enough to have to be put down.

"But beware the law of unintended consequences, for a crazed Queenie could not be contained by the normal measures, and her powerful mass escaped her handlers, killing two grooms in the process. She ran down the hill from the stables to the village. It was market day in the village, and lots of folks milled around the village square, hawking, haggling, and gossiping. At the sight of Queenie, her nostrils flaring, eyes crazed, and powerful hooves pounding, the villagers ran. Anyone too young or too old to run was carried by someone else. The village did themselves proud, and by the time Queenie stood quivering in the village square, it was empty.

"Into this suspenseful scene, a young boy ran out. Apparently, he had left his favorite toy, a spinning top, in the square. His mother was a widow with four young children, the youngest still a babe. At the first sign of trouble, she had taken her young family to the relative safety of the village store, built with wooden beams. Now, though, she yelled at her other sons to hold the baby and ran back into the square to pull her endangered son to safety.

"Seeing the running duo, Queenie charged. The mother and son were far enough away that they may have just made it back to the store, but when she picked up her son and turned to run, the mother tripped, twisting her ankle. Onlookers looked on with horror as Queenie moved inexorably toward mother and son, and some turned away so as to not see the horrific event sure to come.

"But instead of horrified screams, they heard three shots ring out. An actor, Jasper, had shot the horse. He was part of a traveling theater group, and while he was a passable actor, he was quite good as a thief. He had initially viewed the whole situation as an opportunity to take a few coins from unattended booths in the market. But observing the young mother struggling so valiantly to save her son, he grabbed a gun from the gunsmith's booth and shot Lord Hamil's beloved horse." Here the temple brother paused for dramatic effect while Prince Gideon rolled his eyes.

"I get it," Gideon said. "The thief redeemed himself by saving the young widow."

"No, no, that's not the point," Brother Adam said.

"I can't wait to hear it," Gideon said sarcastically, even though he was a bit curious as to how the story turned out.

"To make a long story short," Brother Adam began as Prince Gideon quizzically raised one eyebrow, "Lord Hamil shot the thief, but the thief still held a gun and shot Lord Hamil in defense. Both men fell to earth, never to rise again, at least in physical form."

"Ugh, let me guess. They haunted Crazy Horse Village forevermore?" Gideon asked.

Brother Adam said, "Patience, young man—oh, sorry—Prince."

"Are you mocking me?" Gideon asked with a hint of anger.

"No, I am just asking for patience so I can finish the story," Brother Adam said, unperturbed.

"Go ahead, then," Gideon said ungracefully.

"Well, the souls of the two grooms, Lord Hamil, and Jasper the thief were all judged on the same day by the same spirit. Which souls went to hell and which went to heaven?"

"I don't know," Gideon said, exasperated.

"You are right. We don't know, and since we don't know, we treat everyone as a brother, because we don't know whether we will spend eternity with the man in hell or heaven."

"That makes no sense," Gideon said. "You are living this way so you can go to heaven, whereas the thief . . ." Gideon paused.

"Aw, you see. You don't know whether Jasper went to heaven or hell," Brother Adam stated.

"But everyone is not equal," Gideon protested.

"Oh? Is there a special hell for royalty?" Brother Adam asked.

"You make no sense," Gideon concluded. "Just tell me the rules. I thought you were supposed to instruct me on the rules of this place."

"That is the first rule: treat everyone well," Brother Adam stated.

"Ok, got it," Gideon said as he turned away from Brother Adam, shaking his head, too aggravated to take a nap.

"The specific rules are written on the wall over there," Brother Adam finished.

"What?" Gideon looked, and sure enough, on the opposite wall in large print were the seven temple rules. The first rule was not exactly as Brother Adam stated. It was "Love Everyone As You Love Yourself."

"What if you don't love yourself?" Gideon muttered under his breath and closed his eyes. He only meant to close them for a moment, but he slipped into sleep and a vision. A woman sat in a chair, slightly turned away from him so he could not fully see her face. She wore a pink dress, and her hair fell in dark gold ringlets down her back. Though her body was still, he could see her hands were knitting a red scarf. The unused yarn lay in a bundle beside her on the chair. Gideon recognized he was in the dream in the same room as she, but she didn't acknowledge him. Finally, when the scarf was almost complete and there was little unused yarn left, she spoke.

"Go," she said. "Be brave."

"Private Li," said a demanding voice, interrupting his dream.

"What now?" Gideon groaned as he came awake, propping himself on his forearm.

The man in front of him was tall and massively built, his face a dark brown and his hair completely shaved. Gideon had never seen the man smile during his year of military service after high school.

Gideon sat up fully and said, "Captain, it's been a while. What's going on?"

"By order of His Royal Highness, King Li, you have been ordered to resume active duty in the Seahorse Island Military," the captain said.

"Why did you call me private?" Gideon asked. He had ended his military service as a second lieutenant.

"You've been demoted, and I've cleared your leaving with medical here," the captain replied. "I'm sorry about your nephew, but my orders were to get you on a base and active as soon as possible."

"My nephew?" Gideon asked as he stood, noting the four soldiers who stood ramrod straight behind the captain.

The captain grunted. "Your nephew was born this morning but didn't live long."

Gideon reached for the captain as he swayed at the news. Remembering himself, he dropped his hands and slowly held himself upright. Feeling as though he was held together by frayed twigs, he opened his mouth to speak and then closed it. He took a breath and tried again. "I'm ready, sir."

The double doors to the infirmary blew open as Luke and James came running in. Both men came to an abrupt halt as they took in the soldiers.

7

EDEN, HALFWAY THERE

"I can't believe we're in the upper classes now!" Kaitlyn practically bounced on my hard bed in her excitement. Her hair was sectioned off with big rollers designed to grip hair without pins. With all her bouncing, the rollers were losing their grip and starting the inevitable slide.

Bethany just rolled her eyes and continued with her manicure.

It was the night before our third year officially started. The three of us were sitting in my cramped room, talking about the new school year and getting ourselves ready for the next day. Kaitlyn had a green detoxifying mask on her face that was still wet enough to allow her to talk freely. I was combing my long tangled wet hair into smaller sections, applying hair oil, and then braiding it. The oil application and braiding would cut down on the frizz so I could take my hair down in the morning and place it in a relatively smoother ponytail bun.

For early September, the air was hot and humid, but the sky was blanketed by ponderous gray clouds that signaled heavy rain to come. I had opened the window to let in some air, but rivulets of sweat continued to pour down my face and body, making my scratchy nightgown stick uncomfortably to my skin. It would have been better to open my door to get more air circulating and alleviate the almost overwhelming smell of leave-in conditioner, nail polish, and Kaitlyn's green-apple-scented facial mask. The closed door, however, prevented other girls on the floor from hearing our conversation. I kept my fingers crossed that miniature cameras or recorders weren't hidden in our rooms. As third-years, we had been moved to slightly bigger rooms on the fourth floor.

"What's so exciting about being in a higher grade?" Bethany asked. "We're still in the same place, and we're one step closer to having to share a bed with some old-as-dirt croaker or some other pervert who can't get a woman except by buying her."

I winced, but I couldn't deny the truth of Bethany's words. Our first two years at the school, we had spent hours thinking of reasons why someone would pay two hundred thousand dollars to marry a girl when there were plenty of nice marriageable girls around without the huge price tag. Why was finishing this high school a requirement?

Bethany and I could see no similarities among the girls at school, who ranged from short to tall, from pale white to deep brown, from a little scatter-brained to scary smart. But we knew there had to be a reason for us to be at the Joseph Hyde School for "Exceptional" Girls. Otherwise, why did it matter that Rosemary had switched with someone else?

I had an underlying nagging feeling that we were unaware sheep being groomed for some horrific slaughter. How could I be sure that marriage was the actual plan for me or any of the other girls? Alumnae did not come back to visit the school, and staff were very mum on what happened to girls once they left. I agreed with Bethany that the true reasons for us being at the school, whatever they were, weren't cause for much excitement.

Kaitlyn disagreed. "You don't know that our future husbands will be horrible people. Anyway, we'll find out this year, right?"

Starting in their third year, girls whose bios had secured them an intended husband started exchanging letters with said intended in hopes that such correspondence would lessen the weirdness of going from being a schoolgirl to being a wife for a heretofore unseen male. Kaitlyn found the idea of letter writing to her intended hugely romantic. Bethany hated the whole idea. She said she wanted two more years of peace before she had to deal with a husband. I was in an even stranger position. Apparently, I had an intended, but he didn't want to correspond until I was close to graduation.

I remained ambivalent about the whole marriage thing. I wanted to eventually get married and have children, but the lack of choice chafed more than a bit. Seriously, how could I love a man who chose me based on my interests as a homeschooled middle schooler? Could I respect such a man? I persisted in fantasizing of an escape to another country with my parents and aunt. I wanted a happy life. The uncertainty of life after school sometimes loomed like a dark abyss, threatening to smother any glimmer of contentment in the here and now.

"Are you ok, Eden?" Bethany asked, a small frown line appearing between her eyebrows. Kaitlyn looked worried too. I must have dropped out of the conversation and into my own thoughts, a habit I'd been trying to overcome.

"I'm fine," I said.

I understood their worry. On Christmas Eve of my sophomore year, I finally cracked. Before then, my daydreams of either escaping from school or being home with my parents and old friends got me through the silent gaps in the day when my mind was not focused on schoolwork. When I wasn't daydreaming, I forced myself to focus on my studies so I wouldn't ruin any slim chance of being reunited with my family.

But on Christmas Eve, the horror of the prior Christmas Eve pressed upon me like a crushing stone boulder. No amount of positive affirmation or prayer could lift the boulder. I cried for hours on end. The pain of not being with family was like someone reaching inside my soul and squeezing it until it liquefied and ran down a dirty street drain, never to be seen again.

Kaitlyn and Bethany tried their best to cheer me up, even though they missed their old lives as well. All the girls did. So far, I didn't know anyone who got visitors, which made me think the change of plans in my case happened to everyone. I knew my sorrow was probably no greater or no less than anyone else's. I'd heard more than one girl crying at night. Even so, my grief had me in shackles, and I couldn't summon the will to care about anyone else.

To help me, the school nurse gave me three different types of pills to take daily. She also prescribed a one-hour walk each day. The pills made me so groggy and sleepy that I could barely walk half a mile without feeling exhausted. Without telling the nurse, I began flushing the pills down the toilet. Gradually I felt less lethargic and more like normal.

I no longer prayed as I used to do about my many blessings and the troubles experienced by other people. Instead, I prayed over my own troubles, listing a litany of my worries, fears, and uncertainties. Happiness remained elusive, but through God's grace, I could get through my day-to-day life without completely breaking down. If there was any possibility of reconnecting with my family and living a normal life, I didn't want to take away that possibility by being, well, not normal. Nonetheless, my breakdown caused people to look at me more closely, as if to reassure themselves I wasn't about to go off the deep end again.

"I'm really fine," I said again. "Mrs. Flint arranged for the new language teacher so I can learn Sorean." I was excited about learning a new language.

Bethany looked at me, an odd glint in her eye. "Why did Mrs. Flint do that?"

"I don't know," I said, cleaning up bits and pieces of shed hair now that I was done with braiding. "I think she knew about my interest in doing missionary work and thought I would be interested in learning a new language."

Bethany asked, "Is anyone else taking classes with you?"

"I don't think so. Mrs. Flint said something about learning the language in the side room in the library since I would be the only student," I replied.

Bethany and Kaitlyn exchanged a look, Bethany with one delicately arched ebony eyebrow raised and Kaitlyn with a slight head tilt.

"What?" I asked to their unspoken inquiry.

"Nothing," they both replied, but neither one would meet my eyes. They started gathering their stuff to leave.

"Is there anything wrong?" I asked, confused.

Bethany and Kaitlyn exchanged another silent look. Finally, Bethany said, "We thought for sure you would be taken from the Jade Vine House when you had your problems last year. Kaitlyn was crying, she was so upset. We were happy they decided to let you stay."

"You're not happy anymore?" I asked, even more confused.

"No, that's not it," Kaitlyn said. "It is just that before you came, two other girls had breakdowns, and they were immediately removed from the house. Everybody noticed that you were not removed. We thought it was just because we had Mrs. Flint instead of Mrs. Stout. But now you have a private tutor in something, just because you're interested in it?"

"And you don't have to get shots like the rest of us," Bethany added.

"What are you talking about?" I asked, thoroughly confused.

"Candace, one of the fourth-years, overheard Mrs. Flint telling the school nurse to make sure you received no shots, just the vitamins and the pills," Bethany said.

I hadn't realized that other girls got shots and I didn't, so I just stared at Bethany and Kaitlyn.

"What are the shots for?" I asked.

Bethany and Kaitlyn shrugged. "We don't know. They said it was to help our development," Kaitlyn said.

I was puzzling over this new information when Bethany said, "I think your sponsor is arranging your special treatment." There was an odd note in her voice.

"Special treatment? Taking boring language classes is special treatment?" Kaitlyn asked, incredulous. "Special treatment is a shopping trip!" Since her face mask had set, Kaitlyn's mouth didn't have its usual range of motion, so her words sounded very off, almost like a bad ventriloquist.

Bethany and I laughed, but after our laughter died, it seemed no one knew what to say.

"I'll ask about the shots and why I'm not getting them the next time I go to the nurse's office," I offered tentatively.

Both Kaitlyn and Bethany nodded in agreement. I wondered briefly why they hadn't just asked themselves, but perhaps they figured I had more standing to ask since I was the one missing out on the mysterious shots. In any event, my offer had set the mood in my room back to normal.

"Where is Sorean spoken?" Bethany asked.

"On Seahorse Island," I replied.

"Where is that?" Kaitlyn asked.

"Just south of Sri Lanka," I replied, not sure if that was information I was supposed to share. I learned about geography at home, but it was not covered at school. For goodness sake, we didn't even know where the school was located!

"Oh! Is that the island that appeared overnight?" Kaitlyn asked, her mouth mobile again. She had wiped off the facial mask.

"I think so," I said slowly, trying to remember what I wasn't supposed to say about the island. My father had said that while the island did form superfast, it certainly wasn't overnight. He said no one knew it was forming because of budget cuts at one of the universities. Apparently, a number of positions were cut due to budget shortfalls, but one of the positions cut was responsible for monitoring underwater plate movement. The monitoring technology in place had recorded for years that an island was forming, but no one was around to interpret data. Thus, everyone was surprised when an island the size of Texas appeared so quickly after the submersion. *Was I supposed to know about the submersion?* I wondered to myself. I was pretty sure we hadn't covered it at school.

"I heard the people on that island have the best skin," Kaitlyn continued. "The humidity keeps their skin so soft they don't need moisturizers."

"Well," I said. "Good to know I can forgo moisturizer if I take a mission trip there." We all laughed.

Bethany asked, "How can an island appear overnight? Doesn't it take, like, years and years for an island to form?"

"How would we know?" Kaitlyn replied back. "It's not like we take science here."

After Bethany and Kaitlyn went back to their rooms, I lay wide awake for a long time on my narrow bed, listening to the rain and thunder outside. Every now and then I could see flashes of lightning illuminate the bars outside my window. Eventually, I fell asleep to the thunder.

The next morning, I woke to a bright sun shining through my window. I lay unmoving for a few moments. The storm had chased off the heat, so the air felt less heavy and more like a pleasant breeze. I could hear birds chirping outside and the sound of others getting ready for the day. I finally slid from the warm bed and got myself ready.

As a third-year, I didn't have the option of skipping the beauty room. Putting on makeup for me was like my Art of Conversation class, not easy. I inevitably got powder from blush or foundation on my uniform, my eyeliner was always a little crooked, and my lipstick looked half-baked since I tended to bite my lower lip a little when I was thinking. This morning, however, I was able to do a passable job. As I looked in the mirror to inspect my work, I noticed my face wasn't so round in the cheeks. I had grown a little taller, and my breasts were noticeably bigger. I scrunched up my face in the mirror. My body was becoming more like an adult's, despite my mind's protestations to the contrary.

"Are we ready to go? We should be there a little early to make sure we get three seats together," said Kaitlyn. We were third-years now, so we sat at the upper-class table.

When we got there, I noticed a few new girls at the lower-class table. They had the same shell-shocked look I had when I first arrived. None had bruises. I felt a treacherous shiver of happiness that Giovanni was dead. Appalled at my thoughts and lack of real remorse over such thoughts, I said a quick prayer, asking for forgiveness in my head, and forced myself to engage in conversation. I found that Mrs. Flint's gaze lingered on me for shorter periods of time when I was talking with someone.

"I'm glad it's not so hot today," I said to no one in particular.

"Yes, me too," an olive-skinned, dark-haired fourth-year named Annalise replied as she spread apple butter over a thick slice of whole wheat toast.

"I wonder if the hot weather we experienced is typical for this area," Bethany said.

"I wouldn't know, but considering that those of us who traveled in the shortest time to get here all lived in northeastern areas, I would say the hot weather is atypical." This statement came from a petite honey-blond girl named Jaelle who usually never said a word unless forced to in the Art of Conversation class.

Bethany paused with her fork halfway to her mouth. Her blue eyes narrowed as she looked at Jaelle. I knew what she was thinking. How did Jaelle know where we were from? Other than Bethany and Kaitlyn, I hadn't told anyone where I was from. No one had shared with me where they were from.

Bethany looked around casually. Seeing no teachers within hearing distance and that the girls at the other end of the table were not listening to our conversation, she asked, "How do you know where we're from? Did you see our records?"

"I haven't seen anyone's records," Jaelle replied, a tad condescending. "I just put clues together. For example, Bethany once described how she loved picking avocados as a kid and making avocado fruit juice shakes. Since avocados only grow in warm climates, I know she isn't from anywhere around here."

Bethany started to say something but stopped as Mrs. Flint approached our table.

"Good morning, ladies," she said, smiling.

"Good morning, Mrs. Flint," we all dutifully replied.

When Mrs. Flint moved on, Bethany leaned in slightly and said, "That's great, Jaelle, but what I really want to know is why I'm in this place to begin with and how can I get out."

Jaelle sighed and put down her fork. "I haven't been able to figure that out, especially why we are all here."

"We only have two years left. We have to figure out something!" Bethany replied in frustration.

"What if we all got together and tried to figure out where everyone is from? We could map it out," Annalise suggested.

"But what we really want to know is where we're going," Kaitlyn replied.

"Perhaps someone could break into Mrs. Flint's office and look through stuff?" Bethany suggested.

I was not prepared to go that far, but Annalise surprised us all by replying, "We don't need to go to her office to see what's in her electronic files."

"We don't?" I asked.

"No," Annalise replied. "It's hard to explain quickly, but you know how you can store data on TMDs, transportable memory devices? Well, a lot of times companies and schools and stuff can't store everything on TMDs, but they don't want to build their own server networks. Instead, they store data using someone else's data storage system. We just need to grab one of the teacher's electronic notepads that has access to the GSN before the teacher logs out."

"I like your plan," Jaelle said, sounding impressed.

"I like it too," Bethany replied.

"Is there another network besides GSN?" Kaitlyn asked.

"How can there be another network other than the GSN?" I asked. "It's the Government Sponsored Network."

Jaelle and Annalise looked at me in disbelief.

"There are unofficial networks?" Bethany asked.

Jaelle and Annalise nodded quickly. "But that's not the point," Jaelle said briskly. "We're trying to figure out how to get on the official network, the Government Sponsored Network."

"Won't there be an electronic record?" I asked.

"But that's the beauty of using one of the teachers' notepads. If someone traces the notepad number, it can't be traced to us."

"But wouldn't the teacher get in trouble?" I asked.

"Do you want to know where you are going, or don't you?" Bethany asked, a little sharply.

"I do, but—" Before I could finish my thought, I was interrupted by Jaelle.

"Teacher alert," she warned.

"Oh, Eden, I really like your hair today," Kaitlyn said.

I wasn't as quick-minded as Kaitlyn, so I just sort of stared at her for a moment. Then I felt a hand on my shoulder. I looked up. It was Mrs. Grey.

She said, "Eden, don't forget your first class is in the side room of the library."

"I remember, Mrs. Grey," I replied, smiling and hoping she would quickly move on.

She looked at me like she wanted to say something else, but then she shook her head slightly and said, "Stop by my office after your class."

"Yes, Mrs. Grey," I replied with a tight smile. I was eager to resume the conversation at my table. But as Mrs. Grey turned and walked away, my friends looked at me with weird expressions.

"I wonder if I said I wanted to take a class on local geography if Mrs. Flint would arrange that for me," said Bethany in a snide tone.

I felt as though I'd been slapped. The other girls looked away, including Kaitlyn. Cheeks burning, I looked down at the table. Fortunately, the bell rang, announcing the end of breakfast, and Mrs. Flint rose to give announcements. Stung by my friends' betrayal, I heard nothing of what she said.

When we were finally dismissed, I walked quickly to the library, not bothering to say goodbye to anyone. I was angry that Bethany would make fun of me for the opportunity to take an interesting class, angry that no one said anything in my defense, and frustrated because I suspected that if any other girl had an interest in something not on the curriculum, the school wouldn't arrange an individual class on the topic.

By the time I stood outside the closed door of the library's side room, my anger persisted, but I was also a little afraid of losing my friends over some language I would probably never speak. I wondered if I should dare to ask to be excused from the class and say I just wanted to stick with the regular curriculum. Perhaps that would be the right thing to do?

I knocked on the door and looked around the library. It was sort of small for a library, but then again, most of its books were available electronically through the school's online library. I only visited the library for school assignments for which I needed hard copy books. Today, some girls who looked like second-years were working on an assignment, and the librarian, Mrs. Stillwell, was at her desk, looking as humorless as she usually did.

While I waited for my new language teacher to open the door, I realized I didn't know the teacher's name. It had been a long minute since I first knocked. I wondered if she wasn't in yet. I raised my hand to knock again, but Mrs. Stillwell called my name, causing all heads in the library to look my way.

"Miss Edwards, your teacher is already present. You may go in."

I nodded my assent and then entered the side room.

The room was gloomy, the only light coming from small windows near the ceiling on the opposite wall. I blinked as my eyes adjusted to the darkness. When I took in the sight of the hard-looking man in the room, my stomach plummeted, and fear ran through me like a live wire. My primitive brain took over, and my only thought was to flee.

As I turned to leave, the man spoke. "Aren't you at all curious?"

With my body facing the door and my hand on the doorknob, I said, "Men are not allowed in this school."

"Are they not?" he replied. "I understand that Giovanni and his partner were quite popular."

I bit my lip at the mention of Giovanni's name, my hand remaining on the doorknob, and turned my head to look over my shoulder at the male intruder. He was standing in the corner diagonally opposite me, his body motionless in the way of a snake before it uncoils itself to strike.

"Look, I'm just here to teach you the Sorean language. You are correct. This school doesn't typically hire male teachers, but for some reason, female teachers in this field are scarce." He smiled as he spoke, but it looked as if it took effort.

Though his words seemed reasonable, I felt uneasy. "It still seems—um—not p-p-proper for me to be alone with you," I stammered out.

He nodded. "I see. Your value as an 'exceptional' girl would plummet if there were any indication you were not completely pure. You cannot command such a high price?"

I could sense the same snide tone that I heard in Bethany's voice at breakfast. I bit my lip even harder at the unfairness of it all. *He does not understand*, I thought, *that I'm here because I have no other choice.*

After an uncomfortable silence, I stammered again, "Um . . . I can talk to Mrs. Flint and explain . . ." Here I paused. What would I explain? That I didn't want to take a class alone with a man?

The man sighed and pulled out a small device, pushed a few buttons, and spoke into it, "You were right. Please join us."

At his words, I realized that he spoke into a portable phone, but it was not like any GSN-approved phone that I had ever seen. It was smaller, sleeker, and glossy black, quite unlike the gray boxy portable network phones—NPs—that I was used to seeing officials carry. I also wondered who took his call. There was a heavy silence in the room as I stood at the door. awaiting this new visitor.

After about three minutes, the door opened gently, pushing me reluctantly further into the room. To my surprise, it was Mrs. Abe, the older lady who taught Household Budgeting. I was strangely relieved by her presence.

"Eden," she said with a smile, her voice holding her normal welcoming tone. "I thought being with a male teacher might make you uncomfortable, so I offered to sit in on your lessons. Is that fine with you?"

Surprised at her offer, I nodded my agreement.

"Then let's all sit," she said, gesturing to the table in the center of the room.

The table in question was monstrously ugly and oversized for the small room, a round table with an extremely scarred surface. Instead of table legs, a gnarled and twisted tree trunk served as its support. A silver bowl filled with glittery fake red apples sat at the center of the table. I seemed to remember that decorative fake fruits were a first-year Domestic Arts project.

Sitting at the table, I got a better view of the man. His complexion looked as though he shaved with a rusty knife and washed with sandpaper, the lines on his pale craggy face running deep and dry. His lips were thin and bloodless. I avoided his eyes after a brief glance at them showed his intense displeasure. I imagined him to be about Mrs. Flint's age.

I wondered why he had been hired to teach me. Two years of beauty classes had taught me to recognize quality clothes. He wore a jacket made of black leather. The button-down shirt and pants were both made of black silk. As I sat, wondering why someone with money enough to afford such attire was teaching me, I had the horrid thought that perhaps this man was my intended.

"My name is Jack Holt," the man said, his voice clipped. "I am not your intended."

Startled, my eyes met his. I wondered how he knew what I was thinking. Embarrassed, I blurted out the first thing in my head, "Then who is my intended?"

Mr. Holt's eyes slid away from mine as if annoyed. He surprised me by asking, "Why are you here at this school?"

"I want to make it back to my parents in a way that doesn't bring them shame," I said, speaking the truest wish of my heart. This was my dream, to be reunited with my parents. I noticed the man's fists tighten and wondered why my words didn't please him. I could feel my head starting to throb.

"Which parents do you want to please?" Mrs. Abe asked, a slight smile on her face.

I didn't understand her question. "My parents in Sun—I mean, my hometown. I don't have any . . ." My voice trailed off as I finally got her question. "You mean my birth parents?" I shrugged as I said, "They're dead."

"You're not at all curious about them?" the man asked abruptly.

"I've had no reason to be curious. I feel no lack of love from my parents," I replied.

"Even though they sent you to this god-forsaken school?" He practically snarled at me as his right hand clenched the wooden table.

Mrs. Abe held up a hand to him and said firmly, "Enough."

Mr. Holt pressed his thin lips together and leaned back in his chair.

"Let's start over," Mrs. Abe continued calmly. "Eden, you will take lessons with Mr. Holt for two hours each morning, Monday through

Thursday. You will focus primarily on learning the Sorean language. A little history may be thrown in. Mr. Holt, do you have a lesson plan for Eden to review?"

He looked at her for a moment. "I will have the lesson plan tomorrow morning," he replied as he crossed his arms over his chest.

Mrs. Abe nodded in response, saying, "Eden is quite fluent in Spanish and French. I am sure your classes on the Sorean language will be a pleasure for you both." She then asked, "Eden, do you have any questions?"

I did have one question which no one seemed willing to answer. "Who is my intended?" I asked.

"Doesn't your intended write to you?" Mr. Holt asked. "He might be a better person to ask." The sarcasm in his tone made me suspect he already knew my intended did not write to me. Even those who did write to their intended at the school tended to avoid identifying details.

I said nothing, not wanting to confirm for him that my intended didn't want to communicate with me. I could feel the throbbing in my head intensify.

"If you weren't here, what would you plan to do with your life?" Mrs. Abe asked.

"Ideally," I said, "I would be with or near my parents. I would still like to become a wife and mother, eventually, but in the usual way, where you know the person you're marrying beforehand."

Mrs. Abe smiled at my statement. "If you had stayed at home, you don't think you would have had to be matched by your pastor?"

"I would hope not," I replied.

Mr. Holt just looked at me as though he were thinking of something. He asked, "Why do you have an interest in learning languages?"

"I would like to do some missionary work." I shrugged to show I wasn't fanatical about the idea.

"Does the world need missionaries?" Mr. Holt asked skeptically.

I was shocked by the question. "Of course," I replied. "In many places, they don't know God. Don't we have an obligation to spread the Good News to those stuck in such places?"

"We do?" Mr. Holt asked with a little half-smile on his face. "Mission work is just an excuse to travel."

I could feel my cheeks flushing red at his statement. It was true that travel outside Saved America was limited. Visits to other countries for pleasure were not allowed. Government-related work and missionary work were the only valid reasons for travel outside the country. I knew, however, that I had been curious about missionary work for years. My curiosity began right around the Christmas I had mustered up the courage to ask my parents about my birth parents.

"One last question," Mr. Holt said. "Just out of curiosity, if you found out your birth parents were alive, would you want to meet with them?"

Startled by the question, I started to say no, but instead, I found myself saying, "I don't know."

"That is probably the truest response you could give," Mrs. Abe said with a brief smile. Then she said, "I'm sure you understand the need not to share anything about these lessons in any way. Only Mrs. Flint, Mrs. Grey, Mrs. Stillwell, and I know that you have a male teacher. Just share that you are taking an alternative language because of your personal interest in missionary work. Do you understand?"

Another secret to keep. My father's history lessons, the name of my hometown, and now my male language teacher. I wondered how many secrets one could hold before they started seeping out.

"Why me?" I asked.

"Why not?" Mr. Holt replied with his funny little half-smile as he stood. "I will see you tomorrow, Eden."

Mrs. Abe and I let ourselves out. I wondered how Mr. Holt would manage to leave the school without being caught. I looked at Mrs. Abe and thought about asking her, but I was afraid of being overheard. Plus, her calm demeanor was just as impenetrable as Mr. Holt's caustic energy.

"You have Mrs. Grey next?" Mrs. Abe asked. "I will walk you to her office."

After Mrs. Abe and Mrs. Grey greeted one another, the former moved on to her next destination, and Mrs. Grey and I sat down at the round table in her office. At least a dozen yellow Chrysanthemums held pride of place in the round, squat vase in the center of the table.

Mrs. Grey twirled her stylus she used for writing on the electric notepad. "How was your class?" she asked.

"It was . . . interesting," I replied. "Interesting" was my favorite word for my Art of Conversation class.

Mrs. Grey gave me a tight smile. "You must be happy you get to take a class you have such an interest in."

"Um." I hesitated. "I'm surprised I'm being offered the opportunity."

Mrs. Grey asked, "Is that so?"

I nodded.

"I hope you like it." Her tight smile and frenetic stylus-turning seemed to indicate the opposite.

"Am I doing anything wrong?" I asked cautiously.

Mrs. Grey looked at me for a long measuring moment, temporarily pausing the twirling. Then she answered my question with the same question. "*Are* you doing anything wrong? I will let you answer that question. You see these beautiful flowers?" she asked, pointing to the yellow Chrysanthemums. "They are lovely flowers. When I look at them, I'm reminded of bees. Did you know bees are almost extinct? They exist at this school because it's someone's job to make sure the bees thrive. If the bees thrive, then so do our gardens." I did not understand the switch in topics from me to bees, and my confusion must have shown.

"Confused? Queens can't be confused, Eden. You see, in a beehive, there are a lot of worker bees. I always thought of this school as one full of worker bees. The bees may be young and beautiful, but ultimately, in the grand scheme of things, they are only here to learn how to look beautiful while being a worker bee." Mrs. Grey's lips twisted sarcastically. "But apparently, we have a budding queen bee in our mist."

At my startled look, Mrs. Grey continued. "Do you know what virgin queen bees do after they emerge?"

I shook my head in response, surprised by Mrs. Grey's question.

"They attempt to kill any rival virgin queen," Mrs. Grey said.

I gasped, but Mrs. Grey's expression hardened. She continued on.

"The question, my dear, is not really whether there is anything wrong with what you are doing. The question is, do you have what it takes to be the surviving queen?"

I had reached my limit. Standing up, I shouted, "But I don't want to be queen! Any queen!" I had had it with all the secrecy and innuendos. It could not represent anything good. "I just want to finish school, get married, and see my parents again."

Mrs. Grey stood as well and leaned toward me. "Wake up, Eden. The fight has already begun, and for reasons that escape me, Mrs. Flint has decided to bet on you, risking the entire school."

In her anger, Mrs. Grey's face was becoming a mottled red, her fists were clenched, and her eyes were moist. She looked as though if she weren't so angry, she would start crying.

I started crying, overwhelmed by her anger and my own confusion.

"I didn't ask for anything," I protested, my heart pounding. I had already lost the fight if I didn't know I was in one.

Mrs. Grey shook her head and sat down. I sat down too.

"The decision has already been made. You must study hard and do well. Do you understand? With no slips or hints about your male teacher."

"I will study hard," I said. "But what will happen to me or the school if it gets out that I have a male teacher? What type of fight am I in?"

Mrs. Grey sighed and put her stylus on the table. She picked out one of the Chrysanthemums and started twirling it. "If the information gets out, then others may start to realize that a virgin queen is living here. The more people who know, the harder it will be to protect you—and anyone else living here."

"But—" I began, wanting to know more, but I was interrupted.

"I can't tell you more," she said. "As it is, you probably know more than you should."

"How do you expect me to succeed in whatever it is I'm expected to do if I'm kept in the dark?" I asked, frustrated enough to keep going. "If we are going to be wives, why all the secrecy? Why doesn't anyone come back to visit after they graduate? Why don't I have to take shots like the other girls?"

Mrs. Grey's face had become scrunched up as she looked at me.

I was startled when Mrs. Flint answered my question. "I think Mrs. Grey has provided you with all the information that you—or any of your friends—need at this time. Just trust that we have your best interests at heart," she stated, her tone cool and measured. I hadn't heard her enter Mrs. Grey's office. As she spoke, she placed her hand on my shoulder. I resented the gesture.

I lowered my eyes and nodded my headed slightly. I was having one of those angry moments when I just wanted to explode. I wanted to smash the vase with the lovely yellow flowers against the wall. I wanted to break the electronic notepads. I wanted to yell and scream and cry. Instead, I held still and tense.

"You may be excused," said Mrs. Flint.

I nodded without speaking again and left. I was keyed up with various thoughts scattering around my head like fall leaves during a strong wind. I walked a few feet and plunged right into Mrs. Stout's substantial form. She came around the corner just as I was walking past.

I said, "Excuse me," and tried to move past, but she shoved me back against the wall.

"What were you doing in Mrs. Grey's office?" she hissed, pressing her right hand down on my left shoulder hard enough to hurt.

"I was just telling her—" I started, when I remembered Mrs. Grey's warnings. "I was just making sure I had the right classes."

"You know what? You shouldn't be here at all, not with Giovanni dead." She practically spat the words at me. I could feel her spit sprinkle my face and struggled not to show my revulsion.

"I had nothing to do with Giovanni's death," I said defensively. I looked around, hoping in vain for another person to pass by.

Her eyes narrowed even further as her doughy face leaned closer to mine. She pinned one of my shoulders to the wall with one hand and pressed her other hand, balled into a fist, hard into my stomach. I could barely breathe.

She said, "Everybody in this house thinks they are so damn special! You are not special, you murderers!" Mrs. Stout's hand moved from my shoulder and closed around my neck to squeeze hard. She added her other hand to add more force.

I realized the danger too late as I clawed at her strangling hands. I didn't have the strength to overcome her brute strength. I almost gave in, but I wasn't quite ready to let go of everything in me that lived. My hands, of their own volition, found themselves clenching against Mrs. Stout's face, my thumbs pressing against her eyes with all my remaining strength. I heard her howl like a dog in protest. Then I passed out.

There was only black nothingness, no dreams.

8

GIDEON, ATONEMENT

*A*s Eden escaped into darkness, Gideon lay awake in the quiet of the night. He had dreamed of the knitting girl again. It was almost the same dream as he remembered from two years ago: the same dress, the same turned-away position, and the same glorious hair. But instead of knitting, she held her face in her hands and cried, the vibrantly scarlet yarn forgotten. He watched as the ball of scrunched-up yarn fell from the chair onto the gleaming hardwood floor. It began to unravel as it rolled away.

When he woke this time from the dream, Gideon lay rigid. After the first dream, Gabriel and Lily's baby had been stillborn. Now, Lily was pregnant with twins. And he'd had another dream.

Months ago, when Gideon saw on his watch phone's newsfeed that Lily was pregnant. he had felt relief. He remembered from a conversation with Gabe early in his marriage to Lily that she had stored and frozen embryos "just in case." Given the situation that later arose with Angel and the virus, Gideon had admired Lily's foresight. But after his dream, he wondered if his feelings of relief were premature.

IN THE MORNING, his feeling of uneasiness continued to grow as the coolness of the night gave way to Afghanistan's scorching heat. After showering and shaving with a bottle of water, Gideon slapped on strong deodorant. He reached for his military khakis, noting the new Second Lieutenant insignia. While he had tried to make peace with his demotion, he was glad to be back at his old rank. Last, he reached for his dark shades and went outside to begin his day.

"Lieutenant!" Sergeant Andre Wong said by way of greeting as he approached.

Gideon nodded back, and without further communication, the two men walked in step to Area 10 where they would take roll call before escorting a group of medical personnel to deliver vaccinations.

As they walked, two privates ran past them in a rush, trying to avoid being late to roll call.

"Should we still make them do three extra miles?" Sergeant Wong asked.

"Sounds reasonable," Gideon said with a smile. "Gym tent or outdoors?"

"Gym tent," Sergeant Wong replied in disgust. "Military rule one million and one: no running in dangerous heat."

"I don't recall getting to run in an air-conditioned tent," Gideon said.

"We didn't," Sergeant Wong said. "All these recruits are soft."

"Lieutenant," a voice called out. Turning, Gideon saw his captain wave him over to his tent. He remembered his dream.

"Take over," Gideon ordered Wong and walked over to the captain's tent. It was large enough to fit a large table for command staff meetings.

Upon entering the tent, Gideon saluted the captain and stood at attention.

"At ease, Lieutenant," the captain said as he remained seated and looked at his electronic notepad. Whatever he read made him rub the back of his neck.

"I don't have good news," the captain said.

Gideon felt his mouth go dry, and he braced himself for the captain's next words.

"Your cover is blown," the captain said.

"What?" Gideon asked as his brain scrambled to catch up with the conversation. He was expecting news about family, not him. "Everyone here knows I am Prince Gideon," he said.

"Yes, but everyone here has kept their mouths shut," the captain said as he got up and started to pace. "It's the goddamn media. They had agreed to keep quiet about the fact that you were actively serving," the captain said in an annoyed tone. "But now some Frenchie tabloid has published an exclusive on your . . ." The captain paused in his pacing and used his fingers to indicate quotations. " . . . 'peacekeeping' missions, with pictures."

Gideon swore before exclaiming, "Does this put everyone on the base in danger?"

The captain nodded, his full lips pressed together.

"I need to go back," Gideon said, squaring his shoulders.

The captain sat on the edge of his desk and said, "Look, you are one of my best soldiers. When Wong got captured by the rebels in Bolivia, your special operations team got him out. You took a bullet, but you completed the mission. I could go down the list, but if I was ever in a tight spot, you're a guy I would want to have on my team."

Gideon nodded, not sure which way the conversation was going.

"But I follow the king's order, and his order is that we return you as expeditiously as possible to Seahorse Island."

"When do I leave?" Gideon asked, his throat dry.

"In an hour. Once you land, you still must go through the mandatory decompression period. You haven't lived as a civilian in two years."

"I will return to the island's base?" Gideon asked.

"I think so, but something just came in about that." The captain walked back around his desk and picked up his electronic notepad. He made a small grunt before looking up. "You're going to spend two weeks at the temple instead of the base. A car will meet you when you land."

THE MILITARY PLANE held few passengers, none of whom he knew on more than a nodding acquaintance. Gideon opened his email to begin a message to Sergeant Wong. Leaving so suddenly, he hadn't had time for proper goodbyes. He had only told Sergeant Wong that something had come up and to take over the vaccination delivery mission.

Before he began his message to his former sergeant, he saw he had another message from Gabriel. He touched his screen, intending to move Gabriel's email to the folder with all the other emails from Gabriel that remained unread. This time he hesitated.

Since his conversation with the captain, he had remained in soldier mode. He had packed up, notified the appropriate personnel, and filled in the required forms before heading to the helicopter that took him to the airport. The sight of Gabriel's email hit Gideon like a splash of ice-cold water in the desert, and he shivered. He had to become Prince Gideon again.

With a sigh of resignation, Gideon clicked on Gabriel's message.

Gide—I heard from father that you are heading back to the island. You will be home in two weeks? We are keeping it under wraps for security purposes, but I wanted to let you know that I'm looking forward to seeing you again. It has been too long without you, brother. Mother and Lily ask about you weekly, if not more. They are more worried now that the article has come out on your military missions. Father is only telling them that he is working on it. They will be overjoyed to finally see you again, safe and well. Just a heads up, they don't know the whole situation from two years ago. They and most of the island think you went away due to a drinking problem, so you may want to watch what you drink in public. I know the whole story, and please understand that I don't hold anything against you. How could you have known her nefarious purposes? I just want my brother back.

Seeing his hand shake as it hovered over the screen, Gideon quickly turned off the notepad and went into the small airplane washroom. He cried silently, his back against the door. He hadn't cried in over two years, his grief and pain buried by military discipline. He'd read one message from his brother, and it was as if a balloon popped and all his regret and shame came out in one big whoosh. He had no idea how long he was in the washroom, but he was relieved that he'd finally stopped crying when he heard a knock on the door.

"I got to get in there," a voice on the other side said.

Gideon hurriedly wiped his face and opened the door, to find a major hopping from one foot to the next, trying to hold in his fluids.

"Sorry, sir," he said before retaking his seat.

"Cock-a-doodle-do!"

The captain had said two weeks at the temple. For seven mornings in a row, he had been greeted by the roosters' crowing, and every one of those mornings he had wondered what slow-roasted rooster meat would taste like. After two years of military service, he was used to early risings, but with his return to the island, his nightmares of Angel and her father had returned. They took turns looking at him, pleading and asking him to save them.

In the middle of the night, he would awake with a start, only to see nineteen other guest brothers sleeping on floor pallets. Some lay still and quiet, their limbs relaxed in slumber. Others were not so peaceful. They snored, passed noxious gas, and tossed and turned, lost in their own fretful dreams.

He wanted to scream and bang his head against the wall. Instead, he paced the room until he tired of it. Every night he fell back into an exhausted sleep close to dawn, only to be woken in what seemed like minutes by the roosters' crowing. This morning, though, he could only come half-awake. He slipped back into a light sleep where nebulous dreams filtered through his mind.

"Are you ill?" said an old querulous voice.

Gideon frowned in his sleep but didn't awake from his dreaming. Then something poked him hard, jerking him awake.

Gideon sat up, stretching his arms upward and yawning. He gave a little start as he saw Brother Adam looming over him with a stern expression on his face, gnarled hands clasping a strong wooden cane.

"Did you just hit me with that cane?" Gideon asked, indignant. As he stood up, he realized the room held just himself and Brother Adam. All the other bed mats were rolled up and pushed against the wall.

"I must have fallen back asleep," Gideon said, surprised.

"Ah! That must be it." Brother Adam slowly walked over to the room's lone chair, near the door, and sat down carefully. "You should read Proverbs 6, verses 10 and 11: 'A little sleep, a little slumber, a little folding of the hands to rest—and poverty will come on you like a thief and scarcity like an armed man.'"

"Huh?" Gideon shook his head and kneeled to roll up his bed mat. The guest residence hall was a simple one-story building made with wooden beams. It had one large room for guests, the room stationed between a small kitchen and dining area at one end and a wash and toileting room at the other end. There was an outdoor screened porch that ran the length of the building.

"You missed morning prayers and the morning meal," Brother Adam said.

"Why didn't anyone wake me?" Gideon asked as he stood. "Are the guards—"

Brother Adam interrupted. "I thought you were in the military. Why do you need guards?" The brother shook his head. "I pity the future of this island if the military folks think they need guards."

"I was shot three times . . . Oh, never mind," Gideon said, frustrated he'd been put on the defensive.

"You are missing the real question," Brother Adam said. At Gideon's look of confusion, Brother Adam sighed. His tone was gentler when he continued. "Why are you still burdened by whatever brought you to the temple doors two years ago, drunk and incoherent?"

Gideon looked away, embarrassed at being dissected in such a way.

"I understand that you are not a believer," Brother Adam continued.

"I am a Christian," Gideon said, surprised that Brother Adam didn't know this already. He reached into his shirt and pulled out the necklace with the gold cross his father had given him for his fifteenth birthday.

"But you don't believe," Brother Adam responded. Gideon and Brother Adam looked at each other in understanding.

"May I pray for you?" Brother Adam asked.

"Now?" Gideon asked, feeling like a trapped deer.

"No, I will pray while you get cleaned up," Brother Adam replied.

Gideon nodded as he stripped off his night robe.

Brother Adam's eyes widened, and he shook his head. "I didn't mean you had to get cleaned up in front of me!"

Ten minutes later, a clean and scrubbed Gideon reappeared, donned in the rough gray robe that denoted one as a temple guest. He noticed that he felt less tired. Perhaps the extra sleep did him good. Brother Adam still sat with his eyes closed. Gideon awkwardly wondered if he was still praying for him.

"You have to try to get up on time and attend mealtimes," Brother Adam said, still with his eyes closed.

"Huh?" Gideon wondered why he always sounded like the village idiot around Brother Adam.

"Release from the temple is contingent on the guest being able to adhere to the temple's schedule and engage with others in a positive way," Brother Adam replied.

Gideon grimaced. He should've gotten up on time. "Got it," he said.

"How is your grandmother?" Brother Adam asked, shifting the conversation altogether.

"My grandmother?" He hadn't expected that question. "Why? Do you know her?"

"Not now," Brother Adam responded before asking another question. "Would you have woken up one of the other brothers if he was asleep after the time for waking?"

"Of course," Gideon replied but then thought more carefully. "Well, I would like to think so."

"Yes, you would, wouldn't you," Brother Adam replied in the cryptic way that irritated Gideon.

Once they left the room, Brother Adam nodded to Gideon and the two royal guards posted outside before walking slowly away. Noticing how slowly Brother Adam walked to reach the side door at the end of the screened porch, Gideon wondered why he didn't just retire. Sighing, Gideon trotted a little until he was walking side by side with Brother Adam.

"Since I'm not eating breakfast, I can walk with you and then be on my way," he offered to Brother Adam.

"Ah, Brother Gideon, I won't keel over and die before I get to my desk," Brother Adam replied with one of his wry grins. Gideon noticed, however, that Brother Adam was leaning hard on his cane and breathing heavily.

Embarrassed, Gideon replied, "I didn't think that at all, sir. I'm sure you have many happy years ahead of you." As he heard himself speak, Gideon winced. It was obvious to all that Brother Adam was fighting hard for each day.

To Gideon's surprise, Brother Adam started laughing. It was mixed with some guttural coughing and a few wheezes, but it was a laugh nonetheless. He said, "I guess you learned something in the military after all. You lie like an expert."

Gideon grinned and said, "I'm glad someone finally noticed."

Brother Adam laughed his half cough and half laugh even louder and slapped Gideon on the back. The impact of the slap made Brother Adam lose his balance, and Gideon grabbed his arm to prevent him from falling. One of the royal guards coughed discreetly.

"I'm fine." Brother Adam waved his hand as though shooing Gideon away. "You go on ahead. No sense in you walking with me and then having to come right back."

"You sure?" Gideon asked.

Brother Adam just waved him away again in response. Gideon watched him until he exited the guest residence hall before turning a glowering face to the royal guards. They were dressed in the ubiquitous black suit of the guards and were younger than Luke and James.

"Why didn't you wake me up?" he asked.

The two guards looked at him in surprise before one spoke. "We are deeply sorry, Prince Gideon. On our first day guarding you, I thought you said, 'Do not come into the sleeping quarters unless I am about to die.' Clearly, I misunderstood."

"Then," the other guard said, "the temple brother who just left told us you needed to sleep and to let you rest. We've let Luke and James know you would be slightly delayed. Again, our apologies if we misunderstood the instructions."

"How did you know my life was not in danger?" Gideon asked with his arms folded across his chest, feeling the need to exert some sort of control. "You just believed Brother Adam?"

"The camera, Prince Gideon."

"There is a camera?" Gideon asked, his voice dangerously quiet.

The two guards looked at each other, recognizing that, despite his quiet tone, the prince was not pleased.

"I'm waiting," Gideon said sharply, making no attempt to mask his displeasure.

"Sir!" It was Luke and James. At their approach, the night guards bowed quickly and left.

"Is there a camera in the sleeping quarters?"

"Yes," said James, "on your father's orders. The head brother was not happy, but he couldn't say no to the king."

Gideon felt an unexpected tightness in his throat. His father may not have spoken to him in two years, but the king was responsible for the guards and the camera. Luke and James had taken up their duties as if he hadn't been gone for two years. Apparently, his brother had kept them on his security detail.

"Let's go," he said to them and strode off to the nearby trolley stand. For the past week, they had spent part of their mornings walking around the temple's campus. The buildings were all nondescript and no more than three stories high.

The main services on Sunday were held in a large boxy white square building with a simple cross above its front double doors. It was attended mostly by foreigners on the island, temple brothers, and temple guests. It was also video-conferenced to the island's single prison. Non-incarcerated citizens who attended Christian churches tended to do so in their own sectors.

A slightly less large building sat behind the church and held the offices of the head brother and the other brothers that ran the administrative functions of the temple. To the east of the administrative office sat the temple's guest residence hall. Guests in need of spiritual renewal could stay at the hall for up to forty days at no charge, provided they worked on assigned tasks. Of course, donations were always welcomed. The orphanage for boys sat directly behind the hall. To the west of the administrative office sat the temple's residence hall for the temple's brothers.

Still, with all its buildings, the temple's campus was not large enough to warrant a trolley system. The trolley was needed because the temple shared an extensive farm operation with three other religious groups. To the north of the farm operation was the Catholic Church's center on the island, to the east was the Islamic campus, to the west was the Buddhist campus, and finally to the south was the temple's campus. The temple was non-denominational Protestant but everyone just called it the Christian Church. The farm had been established early on by Steve Li, the island's first king.

As the former king strengthened his hold on the island, religious groups from around the world sought permission to come and do missionary work. The islanders themselves represented a myriad of different faiths. The first King Li was indifferent to religion but not its potential to sow dissent and shift power. As the old South African leader Desmond Tutu noted: "When the missionaries came to Africa, they had the Bible, and we had the land. They said 'Let us pray.' We closed our eyes. When we opened them, we had the Bible, and they had the land."

The first King Li was determined to keep his eyes open and the land under his control. His solution was to allow the sectors to have just about any religion they wanted, provided the religious leaders were native to the island and ten percent of their revenue was supplied to the royal family on an annual basis.

Churches with foreign leaders were allowed if they were limited to the area around the farm and agreed to provide twenty percent of their direct farm yield to the royal family. At the time, the island didn't have their current ability to simply import food. The only churches who took them up on their offer were the four with campuses around the farm, even though, for reasons never fully explained to Gideon, the Catholic Church's Sisters of Mercy operated its orphanage for girls on the north side of the island, far away from the farm.

As the trolley moved languidly along its path, Gideon couldn't help but have a small feeling of awe as he took in the gigantic field before him with rows and rows of edible leafy plants, the orchard brimming with small mandarin trees, the nosy squawks of chicken in large coops, the beekeepers in their strange garb, and farm workers who moved with purpose. The fragrant and foul smells together created an aroma that was earthy and not altogether unpleasant. To Gideon, it seemed like he'd been thrown back to another time.

As a child, he had visited the farm often with Angel and Gabriel. It had been fun to sit in the big tractors when their feet couldn't reach the floor; to run through the mandarin orchard, yelling at the top of their lungs; to eat orange fruit until their small tummies hurt; and to sometimes just lay down, exhausted from all their play, and look up at the hazy sky. He wondered why they had stopped visiting. Did they simply get older and forget the simple pleasures of the farm?

He remembered Angel complaining once about how she hated being an only child. Gideon realized that he had never been lonely. He had always had Gabriel, his twin, friend, partner in crime, and other self. In the military, he was surrounded by men he trusted in life-or-death situations.

Now, though, despite being surrounded by people, Gideon experienced loneliness. He had one week to go before he could see Gabriel, Ya Ya, Lily, his father, his mother, and, hopefully, soon his nieces. He resolved not to screw up this time. He sat up straighter with his arms folded, looking past James and out the trolley window.

"Luke and James," he said quietly, for they were sitting on either side of him.

"Yes?" James responded.

"Let's do our best today," Gideon said.

"What are we doing today?" James asked. "I thought your assignment was to help prep for lunch."

"That is my assignment," Gideon said, hoping his face wasn't turning red. "I just meant that we should do well in all that we do."

"Ok," James said. Gideon pretended not to notice the look James and Luke exchanged.

To cover his embarrassment, he said, "Hey, I think there's a gift shop up ahead. I need to pick up gifts for my return to the palace."

"Ok," Luke replied. "Make sure you do a good job shopping."

"Stop it," James said.

"Sorry, sir," Luke said.

Gideon shook his head at Luke. "I see you haven't learned anything in two years."

Before Luke could respond, a voice yelled out, "Come back here!"

A chicken had fled its coop near the Islamic house and was running headlong toward a field of greens. Gideon had learned in his time at the temple that chickens were never to be let out of the coops. They would destroy an entire field of vegetables if left unchecked. The chicken squawked indignantly as the worker captured him and put him back in the large coop.

As he shook his head at the chicken's antics, Gideon noticed a long line of folks behind the mosque. They were all super thin and dejected-looking. They looked like the drug addicts he had encountered in England but without the jitters. He'd noticed a similar line at the temple recently.

"Hey," he said to James. "Why do the campuses sometimes have long lines of people? Do they come for prayer? Are they recovering addicts?" Gideon had whispered the word "addicts." On the island, illegal drug use was a capital offense. He wondered why those in line were shown mercy and not killed. Maybe they were too young. Some didn't look old enough to be adult age.

A burly man dressed in the blue robe of a temple brother turned from his seat directly in front of Gideon with a look that barely hid contempt. "Those lines are for hungry people who don't have enough to eat."

"What?" Gideon's brow furrowed. "Isn't each sector supposed to take care of its own?"

"Each sector does claim its own, but what that means varies by sector," the man replied.

"Look," Luke said, "the sector heads have to make sure enough food is available for purchase for a lot of people. People who don't have the resources to buy food and don't have relatives, like orphans and the elderly without children, are not at the top of anybody's priority list. Being assigned to a sector just means you have the right to live in a sector."

"It doesn't mean they have the means to live?" Gideon asked.

"Exactly," Luke said.

"But what about the orphans?" Gideon inquired. "Can't they come to the temple's orphanage or the one for girls further north?"

Luke looked at him in disbelief. "Orphans at orphanages have to be sponsored by somebody financially, whether it's their sector or a relative who dies but leaves money for their care."

"And if the sector doesn't want to financially sponsor an orphan?" Gideon asked.

"They scramble for food like the kids you see in that line," the burly brother replied again with a barely civil tone.

"Why are you speaking to me like I'm the one who deserted them?" Gideon demanded.

"Forgive me, brother," the man replied, "but each of the farm's religions has tried to get the attention of The Red Palace on this matter, but to no avail. My bitterness is misplaced." But by his tone, Gideon knew that the bitterness would continue.

"We're at our stop," James said.

As Gideon wandered through the gift shop, his brain was only half-focused on picking out gifts. With the other half of his brain, Gideon wondered about the bitterness of the burly man on the trolley.

"I should have gotten his name," he muttered to himself.

"What?" Luke asked, his eyes focused on keeping track of other customers.

"Nothing," Gideon replied before contradicting himself. "What happens to those kids in the food line?"

Luke continued to look away. "What usually happens to kids with no protectors?" he replied. "It's an embarrassment, really. They say we sell medicines out the front door and children out the back."'

"We've changed since those days," Gideon replied automatically.

"Who's in charge of the sectors?" Luke asked.

"The descendants of those who arrived on the island with King Li," Gideon replied, his eyes widening in dismay as he realized the implications of his statement. "But that doesn't mean the sons are like their fathers or grandfathers. I mean, look at me."

"Exactly," Luke said. "Look at you."

LATER THAT AFTERNOON, still stewing over his earlier conversation with the unknown temple brother and Luke, Gideon started his least favorite chore: cleaning the washrooms. The duty was assigned to him and two other guest brothers. Initially, they had decided one person should do the shower area, one person should do the sinks, and one person should do the toilet area. There was an awkward moment where each wondered who would volunteer to clean the toilets. Gideon surprised himself and volunteered. He thought he was prepared, but each day the smell staggered him anew. Today the smell made him lightheaded. He had missed breakfast and grabbed only a few bites at lunch as he was busy with setting up, serving, and cleaning up from lunch. He was only supposed to help prep for lunch, but the regular brothers in charge of the kitchen were at a food conference.

By the time he sat down at the evening meal, Gideon nearly sighed with pleasure. Two of the guest brothers were chefs in their real lives and had a talent for making simple but elegant meals in the small industrial kitchen they'd been allotted. A cooking range, sink, and a below-countertop refrigerator lined one brick-faced wall, and the men sat at a long wooden table placed close to the opposite wall. Tonight's meal was roasted chicken in a mandarin glaze, asparagus in a cream sauce, small red potatoes seasoned with sage and parsley, and large fluffy rolls with visible steam rising. Gideon prayed that whoever's turn it was to say grace would keep it short. Then he remembered it was his turn.

"Dear God, thank you for this meal," he prayed and then opened his eyes. He took his fork to dig in and then noticed the other men still had their eyes closed.

"That's it," he said. "Please eat."

The conversation was muted as the men satiated themselves on their evening meal. Eventually, though, they began to talk about their day.

"Did you see that long line again?" a guest brother asked. He was one of the two who shared Gideon's task of cleaning the washrooms.

"It's unseemly, the way those young people beg!" This statement came from another guest brother, Segenam. Gideon knew the man's father had gotten him out of several financial missteps.

Gideon covertly scanned the other men's faces. They had that scrupulous blank look island men cultivated when they didn't want their true feelings known. It occurred to Gideon that perhaps no one dared speak out on behalf of those young people barely surviving because they weren't sure how he would respond.

"Hunger tends to take away one's ability to be prideful," Gideon said evenly.

An angry look crossed Segenam's face. "Since when is being hungry an excuse to sin?" he asked, his eyes boring into Gideon's.

Before Gideon could respond, one of the chefs said, "That's not what he said, and you know it. Just eat your cake."

The guest to Gideon's right sighed and said, "Yes, let's have a peaceful meal."

Segenam threw down his napkin and stalked off. Dessert was mandarin-orange cake with a honey-based glaze. It was hard for Gideon to enjoy the cake in the charged silence pervading the dining area. Thinking of the dejected young people standing in line for food and the challenge in Segenam's eyes, Gideon stopped eating his cake after a bite or two. Instead, he sipped his tepid ginger water and reflected on his day.

The next morning, on a walk with Luke and James, Gideon looked around to make sure no temple brothers were around before asking Luke for his phone.

"Why?" Luke asked without turning. "You aren't supposed to have electronics."

"Just give me the phone!" Gideon shout-whispered in exasperation.

"No," Luke said.

"Fine," Gideon said. "You text Gabriel for me."

"Why didn't you just say you wanted to text Gabriel?" Luke asked as he took the phone from his pocket and held it out to Gideon.

Shaking his head at Luke's obstinacy, Gideon texted, "Gabe—This is Gideon. Seeing a lot of hungry young people standing in line for food at the farm. Perhaps we can donate some of our share to feed those without other options? Can you look into it?"

As Gideon was handing the phone back to Luke, a new text came through. Thinking it was Gabriel, he looked, but the message said, "The baby is coming. Can you please meet me at the hospital?" The text came from "My Wife."

"I think your wife is having a baby," Gideon said. "Wasn't she pregnant the last time I was here?"

"Yes, she was," James replied instead of Luke. "She is on her third baby."

"Wow," Gideon replied. "Most women just have one."

Luke's face reddened. "Let me call in a replacement guard."

As the morning wore on, Gideon discovered Segenam had nothing on Luke. Luke was keeping watch, but the rigid way he held his body spoke of his immense frustration for having to wait for the new guard. Gideon was frustrated as well, knowing he was the cause of Luke's current situation. Not the making-the-baby part, but the part where Luke couldn't be at the hospital with his wife.

Their savior came shortly before noon. There was a discreet tap at the back door of the kitchen before it opened to reveal a tall, muscular man dressed in the black suit, tailored white shirt, black tie, dark shades, and professionally shined black shoes of the royal guard. He held out his royal guard badge and said, "Matthew Lang, replacing Luke . . ." The guard paused to look as his watch phone.

"You should've had my name memorized!" Luke interrupted. "Let's go over a few details before I head out."

Ten minutes later, Luke gave a quick nod to Gideon. "Sir, I will see you back at the palace in a week."

"That's fine," Gideon replied. He shook his head as he wondered what Luke's household would be like with three kids under the age of three. With a start, he remembered that there would soon be twin newborns at the palace. It was hard to imagine his brother as a father. *I should have contacted him sooner,* Gideon thought to himself, wondering why he made a problem his first communication with his brother in two years.

Gideon shook off his thoughts and started serving the long line of hungry temple brothers. After the line was gone, Gideon prepared his own lunch. Matthew was standing a little way off, his eyes scanning the dining hall.

"Where's James?" Gideon asked the guard.

"He is checking the perimeter, sir," the guard replied.

Deciding to tease the guard, Gideon asked, "Do all the guards have biblical names? I mean, James, Luke, and Matthew. Should I expect Peter or Mark next?"

"I wouldn't know, Prince Gideon," Matthew said. "I can get you a list of all royal guard names?"

Gideon sighed. "No need." The next week was going to be long indeed.

That night, Gideon fell into another exhausted sleep, but instead of dreaming of Angel or her father, he dreamed of the knitting girl. She was walking on a narrow path in a wooded area in the eerie light of dusk, still in her pink dress. A predator stalked her. Gideon could hear the predator's heavy panting as he ran toward her. He was not stealthy. His feet fell with thunderous power, twigs and branches crunching underneath. She walked on, a bright red scarf around her neck and red headphones in her ears.

Gideon tried to warn her, but no words came out. He tried to move, but like his voice, his body could not follow his direction. The sun's weak light glimmered off a flash of steel. Gideon screamed in his dream and woke up. He put his head in his hands and shook his head in frustration. Taking his hands away from his face, he saw his hands were dripping, not with tears but with bright red blood.

He woke up again, this time for real, and ran to the washroom and vomited. As he clutched the commode, he saw his necklace with the golden cross swinging back and forth. He grabbed it and said, "Lord, if she's real, help her!"

9
EDEN, HISTORY LESSONS

I jerked awake and found myself lying on the hard floor where I'd fallen unconscious. Directly in front of me lay Mrs. Stout, her eyes fixed and unseeing. Blood dribbled out of her open mouth and down her round, squished chin into an ever-growing pool of blood. I realized she was dead.

Hands touched me, and voices called my name, but they seemed far away and removed from me. I reached out with my forefinger and gently touched the red wetness. As I drew my hand back, a droplet fell, causing the pool of blood to ripple in a red wave.

The loud, intrusive voices became even louder. My hand shook, and my vision twisted into a kaleidoscope of red shades. I shook my head to get rid of the red but must have fallen unconscious again, because when I next opened my eyes, I was in the infirmary. A sea of faces surrounded me: Bethany, Kaitlyn, Mrs. Abe, Mrs. Grey, Mrs. Flint, Annalise, Jaelle, and more. Some of them were crying. Too many voices and too many sensations at once. I closed my eyes to stop the onslaught.

"Everyone out, now!" It was the firm voice of the nurse.

When all was quiet, I exhaled a little.

"Eden, I need you to open your eyes," I heard the nurse say. I turned my head away from her voice. I felt her hand touch my face and pushed it away with my own hand.

"Eden, that's enough," she said. "I need to check your vitals. Then I can allow you to rest."

Anger surged through me at her tone. I bit my lip to keep it in check.

"What if she needs to go to the hospital?" said a voice I recognized. It was Jack Holt. I turned my head and opened my eyes, to see him step further into the room. How had he gotten into the infirmary? I stopped biting my lip and started to laugh and laugh. Could my day get any more absurd?

"We can't take her to the hospital," I heard the nurse say through my laughter.

"Look at her!" Mr. Holt shouted. "She needs professional help!"

His shouting made me nervous again. I stopped laughing and started whimpering instead, shutting my eyes to reality.

"Jesus!" Mr. Holt exclaimed.

"We don't take the Lord's name in vain," the nurse said primly.

Mr. Holt made an inarticulate sound, and I could hear them both step closer to the bed. I buried my head further into the pillow, still whimpering. I felt lost and without hope.

"I thought you said she witnessed someone have a heart attack," Mr. Holt said.

"Well, yes . . . that is . . . she saw Mrs. Stout have a heart attack and must have fainted at the sight of the blood coming up," the nurse replied, but her voice sounded uncertain, not her usual authoritative tone.

"You don't sound sure," Mr. Holt probed.

"With her medical history, we're mostly sure, but we're not equipped with autopsy equipment, so we have to guess," the nurse explained with a shrug. "It's just unusual for blood to come from the mouth during a heart attack. I think the sight of so much blood was difficult for Eden."

"You think?" Mr. Holt replied, his usual sarcastic self.

I heard his footsteps come closer. It was hard not to open my eyes when I felt someone standing so close to me. I tried to just breathe in and out, but I was startled when I felt fingers touch my neck, and my eyes flew open to meet Mr. Holt's grim gaze.

"Why does her neck look like someone strangled her?" Mr. Holt said in a tone that scared me.

"Um—" I heard the nurse begin.

"If she dies, if any hair on her head is damaged, I will kill you. Do you understand?" I heard his footsteps walking away.

After that conversation, the nurse did her best. She opened the curtains in the infirmary during the daytime so I could see the gentle slide into fall. I turned away from the harsh sunlight, unappreciative of nature's beauty. She had meals prepared for me that were designed to tempt my appetite, but I told her the smell of such sweet and savory food made me nauseous. I ate sparingly. On days when my crying wouldn't end, she would sedate me, and I had the sensation of losing time. I heard only gibberish when she read to me at night. She continued, undeterred, her voice determinedly cheerful.

This went on, day after day. I was content not to think or feel, only to exist. Mr. Holt, however, had other plans for me.

One night as I started to drift into a drug-induced sleep, I heard the door to the infirmary bang open and heard footsteps coming fast to my bed. Surprised, I opened my eyes. It was my father! Before I knew it, I was enveloped in his arms for a prolonged embrace.

"I've missed you, daughter," my father said, still holding me tight. Eventually, my father loosened his hold a bit, but I gripped him tightly to me again and cried, not whimpering tears but cathartic, loud, and unladylike tears. My father's presence had opened the fault lines in the numb shell that encased me. After my crying eased, my father moved back a little to look at me.

"It's so good to see you," he said, his hand smoothing hair off my face, his own wet with tears. "How is school?" he continued, his gaze holding mine.

"It's so hard being away from home," I replied, tears continuing to fall from my eyes. My eyes pleaded with him to let me come home.

"Daughter," my father said. "You must endure a while longer." I could feel the trembling in his hand as it rested on my head. The lines around his brown eyes were deeper and more numerous than before. His whole frame was thinner, gaunter. Most surprising, my father's hair was almost all gray, no longer a luxurious mane of rich chocolate brown with almost undetectable streaks of gray. The suffering I saw on my father's face made me swallow the plea I was going to make about taking me home. He would take me home if he could, right?

"Where is Mom?" I asked. "How is everything at home?"

"It's fine," he said, his eyes dropping from mine as his mouth tightened.

"Mom?" I inquired.

"Your mother is ill," my father said.

"Are we going to see her?" I asked, sitting up straighter on the bed.

My father held up a hand as if to stop any further questions. "No, I can't bring you to her. You have to stay here."

"What?" I asked, perplexed. "Wouldn't she want to see me?"

"Of course," my father replied, "but it's not possible right now."

"We're going to leave her all alone? We should be with her! Is she contagious or something? What's wrong with her?" The questions tumbled out of me.

"Daughter," my father replied. "Have your mother or I made a decision that wasn't good for you?"

I didn't want to say something harsh and spoil this time with my father, but it was wrong for us not to be with my mom if she was sick. I said nothing in response to my father's question.

My father continued, "Your mother, she . . . well, she needs to rest for a while. She insisted that I come see you. Please trust us. We are doing everything for your benefit. You have to stay here and live well, do you understand?" My father's eyes pleaded with me to say yes.

Instead, I replied, "I understand you sent me here to keep me safe from Inspector Brown. But I'm not sure I feel safe here. I feel more like Jephthah's daughter. Do you remember the story? Her father sacrificed her for an oath. I feel like a sacrificed daughter. Could I not stay somewhere else, Father?"

My father's face became whiter, more bloodless, with each word I spoke. His hand gripped mine almost painfully. "Eden, I swear on everything I still own that if we had kept you at home, you would be in a worse situation." He took a deep breath. "I need you to survive. I need to believe that all the sacrifices we've made mattered."

"Why did you come? How did you even get in?" I asked.

"I came to encourage you to do your best and to let you know that you are very much loved." He squeezed my hand.

I managed a small smile at his words.

My father continued. "Mr. Holt told me things had become difficult for you, and he arranged for me to come. I was blindfolded so I couldn't see the route."

"I'm glad you're here," I said. "Even though I wish I were home with you and mom, I will trust you are doing your best to protect me." I gave him a facsimile of a smile.

Instead of smiling back, my father's expression grew even more serious.

"Daughter," he began. "I don't have much time with you. I need you to remember three things. The first is to pray every day. It is important to have daily communication with God. You need to hear his voice above all others."

I nodded to show I heard him, wondering why he was using this time to repeat basic Sunday school lessons.

"Have you?" he asked.

"Have I what?" I asked.

"Have you prayed every day?" he asked again.

"Um . . . no. Not every day," I said, dropping my eyes and lowering my head, a little embarrassed and ashamed. My father, however, did not reprimand me.

"The second thing to remember is that while your mother and I love you very much . . ." he paused before completing the thought, his fingers tightening on mine almost painfully again. "We really have no claim to you," he finished.

"What are you saying, Father?"

"Your parents are not dead." He had a look on his face that I had never seen, a look of shame.

"But you told me they were dead!" I said, shocked.

"No, we let you assume they were dead, and we never corrected you."

"This doesn't make any sense. How did you get me?"

"We were told initially that your parents were dead and you needed a home. There were some doubts. The demand for babies and toddlers was high, and yet we got you before you even made it to the list."

"So how did you know my birth parents weren't dead?"

"It's not important how. I found out when you were three. I convinced myself you were safer with us." My father looked at me as though I would be upset. He needn't have worried. I felt such desperate happiness to be with someone who knew and loved me after months of homesickness and loneliness that the thought of birth parents seemed unimportant.

"It doesn't matter," I said, shaking my head.

"Eden," my father said, his tone urgent, "from where and from whom we come always matters. I needed to confess this to you now in case I don't get another chance."

The urgency in my father's voice scared me. I let go of my father's hands to give him a tight hug, saying, "You are the father that matters."

I felt my father nod in response, and then he pushed me away gently.

"What's the third thing?" I asked. "Remember to pray, remember I have another family, so what's the third thing?"

"Eden." My father shook his head and gripped my shoulders. "We cannot wish the truth away. How would you feel if no one recognized you as my daughter anymore?"

"That would never happen!" I exclaimed.

"But imagine it," my father insisted.

"I don't want to think about this!" I responded, putting my hands to my ears.

"Eden, your birth parents have had to think about it every day for years. Have some sympathy for them," my father said.

I nodded my agreement, chagrined.

"The third thing is to trust Mr. Holt."

"What?" I asked, completely surprised. "Trust him?"

"Yes, trust me," Mr. Holt said. He stood just on the inside of the infirmary by the door. I had no idea how long he'd been standing there.

"Why are you here?" I asked, resenting his intrusion.

"I am your fairy godmother," he replied sarcastically, opening his arms expansively as he walked closer to us. "I made this touching scene possible."

I viscerally hated Mr. Holt at that moment. I just stared at him, not trying to disguise my dislike, itching to remove the smugness from his face.

"Ah, but all good things must come to an end," Mr. Holt continued.

My father nodded. "Yes, Eden," he said. "It's time for me to return. We should thank Mr. Holt for allowing us this time together."

Thank Mr. Holt for allowing us a minuscule amount of time together after years of separation? I wished I could vent the impotent rage that soared through my spirit! Instead, I gave the briefest of nods to Mr. Holt and turned to my father. I didn't want him to leave, and I started to try to say everything at once. "Travel safe; look after mom; take care of yourself. Oh, what about Aunt Adeline? Is she ok?"

My father held up his right hand to stop my flow of words. "I understand it all, daughter," he said. Then he placed his hand on my head and prayed, "Lord, please watch over Eden. She is a wonderful gift. I pray that you keep her safe from all harm: spiritual, mental, or physical. And please grant her wisdom and the spirit of discernment."

I smiled a little at my father's prayer. To be prayed over by someone who loves you is like someone taking a warm blanket out of the dryer on a bitterly cold day and wrapping you in it.

Then I heard Mr. Holt say, "Are you ready now?"

My father gripped me tighter and said, "I need a brave goodbye."

When I was very young and my father had to travel for work, he would have to peel me off him before walking away. He came up with the idea of giving him brave goodbyes. When he would return days or weeks later from wherever it was he went, he would bring me back "gifts for a brave girl." So, as I felt my father move away, I resisted the urge to cling and just said, "Thank you very much for visiting me."

He nodded and turned away but then said, "Oh, I almost forgot. I have a gift for you." He looked to Mr. Holt and said, "It is just the flower pot you saw me pack."

Mr. Holt nodded his assent, his right hand impatiently tapping his thigh.

My father handed me a plain brown bag and walked away with Mr. Holt.

Before I knew it, the infirmary was empty, and I was left holding the bag. I pulled out the flower pot. It was pink and held fake purple and green tulips secured by a green spongy material. It was an unusual gift from my father. He usually bought me snow globes. The only use he had for plants, fake or otherwise, was to hide memory sticks. Zing! Now I understood my father's gift to me.

As I looked at the artfully arranged flowers and found the hidden memory stick, a part of me wanted to lie down, pull the covers over my head, and continue crying over my depressed, homesick existence. I knew, however, that I would not be able to rest until I had discovered what my father meant for me to find. I was too sad for excitement, but I was curious. The question was, how could I look at the memory stick without being caught?

"Eden, you're up!" It was the nurse.

I gave her a small smile, not sure really what to say. So much had happened in a short period of time.

"Do you want to eat?" she asked.

I nodded and asked, "How much longer do I need to stay here?"

"In the infirmary?"

At my nod, she said, "Well, let's check your vitals, and then I will discuss it with Mrs. Flint."

After she completed my medical checkup, she asked, "Where did you get the flowers?"

I thought for a moment and then said, "I guess a visitor must have left them."

"That was nice of her." Without looking at me, she added, "It's nice that your friends are putting their domestic arts skills into practice."

"Can I have my electronic notepad?" I asked. "I want to see what I've missed. How many days of classes have I missed?"

"Seven."

"Um . . . I will have a lot to catch up on. Hopefully, I can get back to classes soon." I tried to sound sincere.

"I will see what I can do." Before leaving, she said, "It seems your visitors did you a world of good." From the way she looked at me, I knew she knew my visitors were not classmates.

"You should know," she continued, "that arrangements were completed for Mrs. Stout. We had her cremated and sent her remains to her sister. It's unfortunate that she had a heart attack so young." There was a note of warning in her tone.

She needn't have worried. I had no plans to say a single word about Mrs. Stout. I shivered as I remembered the woman's determination to kill me. I figured the divine intervened in the form of a heart attack—or whatever it was—for Mrs. Stout. I should feel saddened at the lost opportunity for her soul to be redeemed, but there was a savage part of me that was utterly incapable of seeing her humanity. What I couldn't understand was why her death seemed to sap the life out of me? *Enough,* I thought to myself. *You must claw yourself into tomorrow and the day after.*

"I understand, Nurse . . ." I started to say and then realized I didn't know her first or last name.

"It's Nurse Wilkins," she said with a small smile.

After she left, I grew anxious to review the memory stick, but I had to be patient and wait.

The next morning, Nurse Wilkins pulled the curtains back, and I didn't flinch away from the sun. She had brought in a tray piled with food, and I ate it all.

"Mrs. Flint is fine with you joining your classes on Monday. That gives you today and the weekend to rest and recuperate a bit more," Nurse Wilkins said. "You can go back to your room tonight."

It was good news, but the thought of lying around all day, waiting until evening, seemed torturous.

"Can I use my electronic notepad?" I asked.

"Oh! I completely forgot about that! It's probably in your room. You can get it tonight," Nurse Wilkins replied.

I nodded my head, but I guess something of my restlessness must have shown on my face, because she told me I could take a walk if I wanted. So, I took a walk in the morning, alternately sat and paced in the infirmary, had lunch, took another walk, and then went back to the infirmary to alternately sit and pace some more. Fortunately for me, my friends interrupted my exciting plans by visiting me.

"I am so happy to see you," Kaitlyn said as she hugged me.

"Me too," Bethany said, hugging me as well so I was sandwiched between them.

"It's good to see you too," I said and meant it. Seeing the two of them made me feel like I was really getting back to normal.

"We were worried," Bethany said. "What happened with Mrs. Stout?"

"Um . . ." I began, not sure what to say. I saw Nurse Wilkins in the background give me a warning look. "I think she had a heart attack or something. I must have passed out."

"Really?" Bethany said. "That's the story you're going with? I thought we were friends." She removed her arm from around my shoulders and crossed her arms, giving me a skeptical look.

"Your friend is telling the truth," Nurse Wilkins said. "What do you want? You want her to make up something to satisfy your voyeuristic interest?"

"No, ma'am," Bethany replied, her eyes lowered. Someone who didn't know her well would think her reddened cheeks a sign of shame, but I suspected it was a sign of anger.

"Nurse," Kaitlyn began, "of course we don't want Eden to make up something. It's just that Mrs. Stout's death was so sudden that we expected a long, dramatic story. I'm sorry we didn't think of how difficult it would be for Eden to relive the experience."

Nurse Wilkins looked mollified and went back to shuffling things around on her desk.

"How have things been going?" I asked Kaitlyn and Bethany.

"The same," Bethany replied with a shrug. She glanced sideways at Nurse Wilkins and whispered, "Let's talk later." In a louder voice, she said, "Let's play the Evil vs. Good game."

"You have the cards?" I asked, incredulous. There was only one set of the cards in the whole school, and you had to check them out of the library. My parents had never allowed me to play, so when I saw it was available via the school library, I had immediately added Bethany, Kaitlyn, and myself to the waitlist. The game was perfect for three players. There was a judge, an "Evil" player, and a "Good" player. If you didn't want to do the "Evil" or "Good" deed on your card, then the other players could pop you on the forehead with a finger flick.

"I have the cards," Bethany said with a smug smile. "The school hasn't pulled it yet."

"I explained to the librarian that it helps girls distinguish between right and wrong," Kaitlyn said, her face as guileless as ever.

"Whatever," I said. "Let's play."

The game was as fun as we thought it would be, some of the cards causing me to laugh out loud. Unfortunately, it seemed we had just started when Nurse Wilkins told Kaitlyn and Bethany that visiting hours were over. A glance at the window showed that daylight was losing to autumn's longer nights. We had been playing for over an hour. I thought about the memory stick.

"Can I go to dinner with my friends and then go back to my room?" I asked Nurse Wilkins.

"Sure," she said. "You don't have to wait until later."

I was comforted by the ritual of dinner. I wasn't hungry, but I had missed being around my friends and having a routine to ground me. There were no real earth-shattering conversations. Annalise and Jaelle told me they were happy to see I had recovered. I smiled at their words. I didn't say that I hadn't really recovered, that I hadn't processed a single thing that had happened to me in the last two years. I didn't want to find out what would happen if I couldn't keep it together again. I wished I could have a heart-to-heart conversation with Bethany and Kaitlyn and tell them everything that was going on. But I had to hold my secrets, no matter how heavy they became.

"You want to come to my room after dinner?" Kaitlyn asked, her face alight with curiosity and concern.

I thought about the USB. "I do, but I'm so tired I should probably go to bed early," I said. "Maybe later this weekend?"

"Sure," Kaitlyn replied, reaching across the table to give my arm a small squeeze.

"Yeah, you should take the time to rest," Bethany said. "You don't look so good."

"Thanks . . . I think," I said.

Annalise and Jaelle looked at Bethany incredulously.

"Well, I'm just being honest," Bethany said defensively.

Brushing my teeth later in the evening, I had to give Bethany points for honesty. I felt a lot better, but I looked like I had been sick. My clothes fit looser on my thinner frame, and my face looked older. I shrugged and went to my room. I was sure I would have no trouble putting the weight back on.

Once back in my room, I plugged in the USB, wondering with anticipation what it would reveal. On the screen, my mother lay in a hospital bed. She looked terribly ill; ravaged would be a better word. Her hair was gone, only a few wisps remaining, and her frame was skeletal. She wore no makeup, not even lipstick. Someone off-camera was talking with her.

"You don't have long," the off-screen male voice said. Was my mom dying? The man's voice was soft, with well-modulated tones. My brain tingled. I had heard that voice before, but where?

My mother nodded. "I know," she rasped.

"You are not afraid?"

My mother just shook her head and smiled. I smiled back at her a little, happy in some small way that I was getting to see her face and hear her voice, even if under horrible circumstances.

"You aren't afraid for your daughter? We can help her reform her sinful ways if you just tell us where she is."

I gasped. It was Mark Brown's voice.

"Inspector Brown," my mother said. "I know this world is full of Rachels. I know that Eden is a Leah." My mother paused to catch her breath. "God will place her where she is meant to be."

"You don't know where she is?"

My mom shook her head, and her eyes closed.

"Then you are of no further use to me, are you?" Inspector Brown said, moving into the camera frame for the first time. His voice was almost a whisper, but his body was stiff, his face suffused with red rage. His right hand reached out for my mom's throat.

I gasped.

My mom opened her eyes and smiled.

I shook my head. "Mom," I whispered, my hand touching the screen.

"You're smiling?" Inspector Brown asked, my own unasked question.

My mom closed her eyes and seemed to exhale.

Now, instead of strangling my mom, Inspector Brown grabbed her shoulders and shook her. When she didn't respond, he moved away, his face revealing extreme frustration. "Damn you!" he shouted, his fist hammering at the air above him.

"What's wrong?" I heard another voice say, followed by the sound of a door slamming shut. The voice was female.

"She's dead. This ungodly woman up and died on me," he said, kicking the bed.

I stopped the video and closed my eyes, feeling the grief well within me.

"I guess this is a dead end, then," said the other voice with disappointment. I hadn't stopped the video like I thought. The tears running down my face had fallen on the notepad, which was gripped tightly between my hands. I couldn't speak clearly enough to give an oral shutdown order to the notepad.

"You know . . ." Inspector Brown began pacing the small room. "This is not a coincidence."

"What do you mean?" said the unknown woman.

"That girls like Eden are disappearing," Inspector Brown replied.

"You think they're being kidnapped?" said the female voice.

"No, I don't think so," Inspector Brown replied. "I don't really think Eden was kidnapped. Do you notice how all the royal families—east or west—never have to use surrogate genes or wombs? And they have no defectives? It's as though the virus never touches them at all."

"They know which girls will not require the use of a surrogate?" the female voice inquired. "But's that's impossible. Plus, the male could be the problem."

"Maybe," Inspector Brown said, pursing his lips.

"Well, who do you think is the middleman, the broker between the girls and the families?" The woman's tone had changed.

"It was supposed to me!" Inspector Brown kicked the bed again, and I felt my heart skitter inside the numbness.

"How unfortunate," the woman said.

I saw Inspector Brown jerk and then slide to the ground, his mouth a perfect O of surprise. He lay unmoving on the floor beside my mom's bed. I heard footsteps and the quiet closing of the door.

That night I didn't dream, but I remembered. With an almost visceral hunger, I remembered the mother for whom I longed. I remembered her rinsing our hair with scented water so that while learning my lessons, I would randomly catch a scent of jasmine, rose, lavender, or whatever other flower we were growing at the time. I remembered that she never sat still for long. She was a body in motion—cooking, cleaning, sewing, or doing something—yet her motions were graceful, never hurried. I remembered her narrow hazel eyes framed by thick brown lashes, chestnut-brown hair mixed with gray, and white alabaster skin so different from my own. The person I saw in the video was a shadow of her former self. I hungered all night for a mother's love that would never return to me.

In the morning, I took off my necklace and gripped the cross as tight as physically possible. I heard a snap and felt pain in my hand. I opened it to find the cross had cracked, and my skin had been pierced by the two jagged edges. As I looked at the slivers of blood, my vision went red. It was as if I saw my room through a red gauzy veil. I closed my hand and didn't look again until I had washed it all away.

10

GIDEON, THE RETURN OF THE PRODIGAL SON

G ideon sat on the ground outside the guest residence hall, his back against the wall. His fingers randomly pulled threads of sparse grass from the ground as he remembered his dream. He couldn't shake an ominous feeling. He had dreamed of the knitting girl the day Lily lost her first baby. If the dream was connected to Lily, should he even return home?

"Ugh!" Gideon stood up, wiping the dirt from his hands and pants. He strode off and walked around the campus. It was midafternoon on a Sunday. Church service had let out a couple of hours ago. Now the farm was mostly quiet, but a few groups of men sat outside, talking and laughing with one another. Gideon ignored them as he walked at a fast clip around the campus. Perhaps the men sensed his mood, for though they nodded respectfully as he passed, no one asked him to join them.

Gradually, Gideon slowed his pace. He felt a twinge of guilt as he caught sight of Matthew and James in his periphery but decided to walk a little further before he turned and walked backed to the hall. By the time he returned, day had slipped into early evening, and it was almost time for dinner. Giving his guards a nod, Gideon continued inside without them. He was grateful the walk had calmed his ping-ponging thoughts, but his heart still felt disquieted. He sighed when he spied Brother Adam sitting in the lone chair in the room.

"Eh, you're finally back. I thought I was going to have to send out a search party," Brother Adam said, looking relieved.

"Is anything wrong?" Gideon asked.

"Segenam's gone. We don't know where he went. You're the only other one who was unaccounted for. The head brother is going to say something at dinner tonight. He asked everyone to come fifteen minutes early." Brother Adam slowly stood up. "I'm glad nothing happened to you."

Surprised to see that Brother Adam had worried about him, Gideon was further surprised by James and Matthew bursting into the room, guns drawn.

"Pack quickly," James said. "We leave in ten."

"Why?" Gideon said.

"We have orders to head for the palace immediately."

"What?" Gideon said, almost shouting.

"Talk on the way," Matthew said. "Pack now. We have to go."

Matthew and James were in full guard mode, constantly scanning the room and speaking through their watch phones to other guards. By the harsh set to their faces and the way they were speaking to him, Gideon knew they thought there was some real threat. He packed his few belongings and was ready in five minutes.

Matthew and James stopped him as he reached for the door to go outside. Instead, a plethora of royal guards came in, surrounded him, and rushed him so that he was almost running to the car. Once in the car, he looked around and saw about twenty armored black SUVs and various police vehicles with flashing lights. James sat in the passenger seat up front, and Matthew was next to Gideon in the back.

"Wait," Gideon said. "What about Brother Adam?"

"In another vehicle," James said at the same time Matthew shouted into his watch phone, "Go, go, go!"

"What's going on?" Gideon asked.

"Stay down, sir!" Matthew shouted and then forced his head down.

"I thought the vehicle was armored!" Gideon shouted back, trying to force his head back up.

"It is, but we don't want them to see which vehicle you're in," Matthew said.

Thoroughly confused, Gideon kept his head down and tried to get a sense of what was going on.

"I got three mercs!" said a voice through James's watch phone.

"Good job," returned James's calm voice. "Any others?"

"Don't know; still looking. The ones we caught had smoke grenades."

"My phone is flickering," Matthew said, his hand still pressed hard on Gideon's head.

Gideon's eyes widened as he realized the possible implication.

Before Gideon could say anything, he heard James shout, "All non-Faraday cars pull out of formation, now!" Gideon could hear a murmur of voices through both Matthew's and James's watch phones.

"Do it now!" James shouted again. A few moments later, there were only five vehicles moving, with the one containing Gideon right in the middle.

"Anybody there?" James asked. Only the four cars surrounding the one with Gideon responded.

"Storm? Daniels? Raven?" James tried to connect with the other cars, but no one responded.

Gideon pushed away Matthew's hand and sat up. "I think they know by now which car I'm in." Pulling up the backseat computer, his fingers moved quickly over the keyboard.

"If we lose visibility, shift the car to screen mode." He leaned and twisted to direct his statement to the driver.

"Was that an EMP blast?" Matthew said, looking at Gideon.

"I think so," Gideon replied. "Tell the drivers surrounding us to have screen mode ready with this car controlling."

"Sir . . ." Matthew began.

"That was an order," Gideon commanded.

"Support in all vehicles have screen mode ready, my car leading," James ordered via his watch phone. To Matthew, he said, "Remember the U.K. Prime Minister." The prime minister had been assassinated after an EMP blast knocked out all the electricity in a one-mile radius surrounding her armored car detail.

Gideon looked around and realized that despite the blast, he could still see a great deal as the lights were out only in the area he was in. The EMP blast must have had a small, targeted radius. Realizing that he was the target, Gideon could feel anger sliding along each of his nerves. The emotion gathered strength as it traveled through him.

"How many miles until Geyser Park?" James asked. "That will be one of our blind spots."

Shaking off the anger, Gideon focused on the screen in front of him. They were almost to the park.

"We have less than ten minutes," he said to James.

"Switch to screen mode," James commanded via his watch phone.

A boom sounded, and the car was shrouded in darkness. Wisps of smoke began to fill the car.

"I have no visibility," said the driver, coughing. "I think that was a smoke grenade." All the cars began slowing down.

"Screen mode!" James commanded, his voice sounding strangled. The smoke was heavier, but to open the windows would expose them to even more smoke.

With screen mode, Gideon had control of the car. He controlled it as though he was playing a video game, using his fingers to go forward or turn. With a touch of his fingers, the car was flying at just over two hundred miles an hour, and the cars surrounding him followed suit. A layout of the road was on his screen.

The one negative of the program was that it couldn't detect obstacles on the road until the car was less than five miles away, which, considering how fast they were going, didn't give him much time to react.

The screen began to make a warning sound.

"What is it?" Matthew said, tense.

Gideon said, "There's a large roadblock ahead. I'm reversing course." As his fingers flew over the keyboard, he heard another boom and looked up, to see a flyaway piece of metal strike the windshield. The windshield didn't shatter, as it had been designed to withstand such things. The car that was now in front of them had not been so well-designed. It was a mess of shattered glass and misshapen steel.

"Should we check to see if anyone survived?" Matthew asked, even though Gideon had reversed course and the cars were moving backward.

"Already done," Gideon said, staring at the screen. "Systems show no signs of life."

The cars moved awkwardly as they made their way backward up a nearby down ramp.

"Drivers, take over," James commanded once all the cars had made it up the ramp. He pushed a button so the siren would sound, and all the other cars did the same.

The drivers turned the cars around to face forward, and they were quickly met by a company of other vehicles. Through the flurry of voices coming through on James's watch phone, it became clear that the other vehicles represented the rest of Gideon's security detail.

Arriving at the palace, Gideon was again surrounded and rushed inside. As the other guards left him, Matthew and James remained, but instead of a group of three men, there were four men. Brother Adam was the last of their quartet. He was doubled over and wheezing.

"I will call for medical," James said, looking at Brother Adam with concern as he lifted his wrist.

Brother Adam waved his hand to indicate for James to hold off as he glared at Gideon.

"You call . . ." He paused to suck air down his throat before he continued. "You call that driving!"

"I wasn't just driving. I was trying to stay alive," Gideon retorted. "And sit down before you keel over."

It was a testament to how tired the brother was that he did exactly as Gideon said.

Gideon realized he would have to see what accommodations could be made for Brother Adam. It was already evening, and Gideon wanted to find out what was going on before he sent the brother on his way.

"Gide!" a voice called out.

Turning, Gideon saw his brother walking toward him with his arms out. Gideon was enveloped in a bear hug which he returned whole-heartedly. Both the brothers' eyes were damp when they finally released each other.

"I am so glad you're here!" Gabriel exclaimed, reaching out to give his brother's shoulder a squeeze. "Even if that idiot Segenam is the reason."

"He was behind the attack?" Gideon questioned.

Gabriel looked at the guards and said, "The king wants an update immediately. Let's head over."

"Brother Adam . . ." Gideon began.

"Is making himself quite comfortable," his brother responded. "Look over there."

Gideon looked and saw a staff member leading the brother away, deeper into the palace. The staff member was walking, but Brother Adam was riding a smartly designed red-and-silver mini-scooter intended for individuals with limited mobility.

Gideon shook his head and then fell in step with the other three men to walk toward the king's offices. Gideon had been expecting more of his family to greet him, but all he saw was security personnel. No one looked at him askance, and they bowed respectfully as he passed. Although, he supposed the respect could have been for his brother. Nonetheless, his day was ending very differently than he expected. The adrenaline from the car ride was wearing off, causing his hands to shake, so he fisted them.

As they continued walking toward his father's offices, Gideon noticed the difference in lighting. While the palace was carved out of mountain stone, slanted skylights toward the front part of the roof let in much-needed sunlight during the day and an arresting blend of star and moonlight at night. Sometimes as a boy, he would stand underneath the skylights and just stare at the night sky, mesmerized. For privacy reasons, the glass was one way so those inside the palace could see through the glass to nature's vibrant wonders but those on the outside could not see inside the palace. Tonight, though, the skylights were covered in specially made heavy curtains, blocking out all light.

Someone had turned on extra lights inside to offset the darkness, but the light seemed artificial and jarring.

When they arrived at the king's office, Royal Assistant Joseph Park motioned for the guards to sit in the waiting area and said to Gideon and Gabriel, "They just got started. You aren't too late."

Not too late? Gideon thought to himself as he and Gabriel walked into the king's office. The brothers stopped at the sight that greeted them. Their father was not alone. Seated with their father around the conference table were the king's chief of staff, the minister of internal security, the minister of communications, and a nun. To Gideon, the nun looked familiar, but he couldn't quite place her. Everyone stood when he and his brother entered the room.

"Please excuse us," the king said to the people at the table.

They all quickly exited, leaving the king alone with his sons.

The king stood and gave Gideon a lengthy hug before pulling back, still holding on to Gideon's arms. "Are you well?"

Gideon nodded. "Yes, Father."

"I'm glad you're home," his father said before releasing him with a final pat on the arms and sitting back down. "Unfortunately, we have to deal with this emergency before celebrating your homecoming."

The meeting began again with the addition of Gideon and Gabriel. Gideon's head was swimming from how quickly things had moved in the last few hours. He felt uncharacteristically unsure of what to do or say, like a little kid sitting at the grown-ups' table for the first time. From want of something solid to hold on to, his hands gripped his knees under the table.

"As I was saying yesterday," Gabriel began, "thanks to Gideon, we now know about the sex trafficking ring Segenam was managing." He avoided looking at Gideon's shocked expression.

"How many kids are involved?" the king asked.

The chief of staff shook his head and grimaced. "Using conservative estimates, about a thousand, sir."

The folks seated at the table gasped almost in unison. Immediately, everyone began talking at once. "Impossible!" "That much?" "How sickening!" and so forth.

The king banged his hand on the table to restore order. Once the table quieted, he turned to the chief of staff and said succinctly, "Explain."

Yes, Gideon thought to himself, *please explain.*

The chief of staff replied, "Once Gideon alerted us to the youth standing in food lines, we did some digging."

"Why was nothing done before?" Gideon interrupted, remembering the brother from the trolley at the farm who was upset that The Red Palace hadn't responded to reports of hungry kids.

"It's simply not our job," the chief of staff replied. "Sectors are expected to take care of kids without guardians or parents in the same way as they are supposed to care for the elderly without relatives."

"But that is not what's happening," Gabe said, as he turned to look at Gideon. "After I got your text, I discovered it wasn't a simple issue. On paper, the sectors are doing exactly as expected. They pay a fee to the usual charities to have such children trained in a marketable skill. The expectation is that they won't become rich, but they will be able to support a moderate lifestyle."

"Selling sex?" the minister of communications asked impatiently, arms crossed over her chest.

"Wait," Gideon said, holding his hand up for emphasis. "I hate to sound like a playlist on repeat, but the training requirement was put in place years ago to avoid this type of situation. And we get reports every year on how much the sectors spend on training. What happened here?"

His brother replied, "We get the combined dollar amount from all the sectors but not the per sector amount or the amount per kid. But once we compared birth record data with the number of kids in training programs and in the school system, we realized that there are a whole lot of kids that are simply unaccounted for."

"Unfortunately, truer than it should be," the minister of internal security said. He was a few decades younger than the chief of staff and about a decade younger than the minister of communications. "We've discovered, thanks to Prince Gideon, that for the most part, the kids who make it to a charitable training school are trained. There are a few problem charities, but most of the charities do what they say they do.

The problem is the kids who don't get to a reputable training organiza-tion. The best case, at least for a special few girls, is they get sent to a school in Saved America which specializes in training girls to be brides. While we've known about the school for years, it is only recently that we discovered that placement is not always voluntary and that some girls are trained to be companions. Our intelligence agency missed that fact."

"Or maybe they decided not to share it," the chief of staff said, glancing at the king with a look Gideon couldn't decipher.

"Does it matter if it's voluntary or not?" the minister of communica-tions asked. "It is just plain wrong for a fourteen-year-old to attend a training school for brides or, worse, companions."

"There's nothing wrong with training girls to be wives," the minister of internal security replied with a puzzled expression.

The minister of communications stared at him incredulously. "You really are as clueless as they say you are."

The king interrupted their squabbling. "What happens in the worst case?"

"Worst case, they're sent to brothels which cater to a certain clien-tele. Thankfully, the brothels are in Thailand or in some other country and not here," the minister of internal security replied, still red-faced from his exchange with the minister of communications.

"I'm not sure the location matters to a child who's being raped," the nun said. Her rebuke was spoken in a low, mild tone, but the minister of internal security's face still flushed a deeper shade of red.

"Perhaps it's time to make an example of Segenam and anyone else who's involved," the chief of staff said. "Our analysts figure that eighty-six percent of those involved in domestic terrorism come from unclaimed youth. We need to cut off this tree at the root."

"First, we need to make sure we have an alternative for these kids," the king said. Turning to the nun, he said, "Abbess Turner, can your organization handle the logistics involved in taking care of this island's unclaimed children, including the ones who have not been trafficked?" Switching to look at the chief of staff and minister of internal security, he asked, "How many kids are in this latter category?"

The minister of internal security shook his head with an embarrassed look on his face, but the chief of staff calmly said, "We are working on getting final numbers to present."

"Good, get it to me as soon as possible," the king said before turning back to Abbess Turner. "Based on what we know today, could your organization handle this task?"

"We could, but we would need to bring in foreign help," she replied, looking at the king.

The table fell silent as everyone considered her words. To bring in foreign help would be unthinkable, but the Abbess couldn't save each unwanted child. She was busy enough overseeing current placements at the temple and the Sisters of Mercy.

As the silence stretched out from moments to minutes, Gideon fought the childlike urge to fidget. The chief of staff sat confidently, his salt-and-pepper hair cut short and expertly layered, not a strand out of place. The minister of internal security played with an electronic pen as he waited like a quivering hunting dog for his master to release him for the hunt. The minister of communications sat with her back straight, her dyed red hair pulled back into a bun secured with an antique hairpin, waiting to spin what needed to be spun. The Abbess sat quiet and serene, accepting the outcome of the meeting, even as she waited for the king's verdict. Gabriel sat looking at his father, but Gideon couldn't gauge his father's expression.

Finally, the king said, "Shut down the problem charities immediately. The minister of communications shall appeal to the good hearts of the island's citizens and request on behalf of the royal family that a home be given to unclaimed children. The royal family itself will bring in one such child as a ward."

Gideon and Gabriel looked at their father, mouths agape in surprise. "Have you talked to Mom about this?" Gabriel asked.

The king held up his hand as if Gabriel's comment was of no consequence and said to the minister of communications, "Work with the finance department to figure out an affordable monthly stipend that can be given to each family."

"That's very generous of you, Father," Gabriel said, even more surprised than before. He looked at Gideon, who looked back at him. Their father was notoriously stingy with money.

"Now for the hard part," the king said. "What to do about Segenam and his affiliates."

"Sir," said the chief of staff. "I received word during the break that Segenam died in the car chase involving Prince Gideon. His car flipped over when he tried to block Gideon on the road."

"Well, at least that's one problem taken care of," the king said. "I would have ordered execution for the man who almost murdered my son brazenly, but it would have been most politically inconvenient. This way is a lot easier."

Gideon kept his face stone-like, but inside he was sinking. Segenam tried to kill him just so he could keep trafficking children? It was a sickening thought and didn't make sense as the car chase wasn't exactly discreet. As he thought about it, he concluded that the most likely reason for Segenam trying to kill him was revenge for exposing his secret. That thought was disturbing too. He wasn't sure what would have happened had the EMP blast worked and he'd been surrounded by Segenam and his men, but the odds weren't good that he would have survived. On the flip side, he wasn't sure what would he have done if the car systems had reported signs of life in the mangled vehicle. Would he have helped? Recognizing that his thoughts were spiraling, Gideon took a deep breath.

Gabe gave him a sympathetic look, and Gideon felt some relief that he could discuss things with Gabe later.

"His affiliates?" the minister of internal security asked, his hands no longer twirling the pen.

"Execute them all," the king said. "The royal executioner is back from vacation."

"Yes, sir," the minister replied, the hunting dog within him standing up on hind legs and barking in eagerness.

Sighing, the king turned to his chief of staff. "For those citizens abroad who are involved in this business, try to get them extradited back here to the island. Otherwise, work with intelligence to have them taken care of in place."

"Yes, Your Highness," the chief of staff replied, his mind less hunting dog and more that of a master chess player strategizing his moves, trying to stay two steps ahead of his enemies. "There may be repercussions," he continued.

"Yes, Segenam's father is influential," said the minister of communications. "He is head of the largest sector, with extensive business connections in China, the United Koreas, and U.S.S.A, or Saved America."

"I think he wants to make a match between Gideon and his daughter," added Gabriel.

The king shook his head. "She is not a good fit for this family. I have someone else in mind for you," he said, looking at Gideon before turning to his chief of staff. "The arrangements are being taken care of?"

The chief of staff nodded slowly before saying, "I spoke with Jack. We had to move the timing of things up a bit, but everything is falling into place."

The king's brow furrowed, and he said, "Good, but schedule time to update me on the situation."

"Yes, sir." The chief of staff nodded.

Gideon looked between the two of them. It wasn't uncommon on the island for parents to heavily facilitate the marriages of their offspring, but normally their children knew upfront what was going on. He wasn't aware of any such marriage discussions, but maybe his parents felt the need to step in after the Angel debacle. All he knew was that this day needed to end soon. He wasn't sure how much longer he could maintain the stoic façade. With relief, he noticed his father take a breath and place his hands on the table, a sign that he was about to end the meeting.

The king said, "I want it to be clearly understood that Sector 16 is no longer in favor. The sector will receive no royal grants for the next year." There was silence at the table as everyone considered this unprecedented sign of royal rebuke.

"That would punish the entire sector, though," Gabriel said. "Not just Segenam's family."

"Exactly," the king responded. "Once it is clear the sector is no longer in favor, the sector will most likely appoint a new leader, someone other than Segenam's father."

Gideon happened to glance at the chief of staff as his father spoke. A smug look crossed the man's face so quickly Gideon would have missed it had he not been looking directly at him. He remembered with a start that the chief of staff was a member of Sector 16. The chief of staff wouldn't try to become Sector 16's new leader, would he?

After the meeting ended, Gideon and Gabriel stayed behind with their father.

"Gide, how was the military?" Gabriel asked. "Lily asks about you all the time."

"She must be due soon?" Gideon asked.

Gabriel looked at him in open-mouthed surprised, and then he and the king started laughing.

"She had the twins a few days ago!" Gabe said. "I didn't realize you didn't know. I assumed father would tell you."

"And I assumed Gabriel would tell you," the king said, shaking his head and smiling. "We should have told you."

"You think?" Gideon asked and immediately regretted his snide tone. "I can't wait to see them. Hopefully, they take after Lily."

"They are absolutely perfect!" Gabriel enthused, missing Gideon's little joke entirely. "You have to see them!" Gabe then proceeded to show Gideon picture after picture of his perfect girls.

"Do they have time to eat?" Gideon asked. "It seems they're getting pictures taken every waking moment!"

"I didn't take pictures of that," Gabriel replied, embarrassed. "Lily doesn't like me taking pictures of her breastfeeding, even though—"

"Gabe!" their father interrupted.

"Sir!" Gabe replied, startled.

"Gide will see my beautiful granddaughters tomorrow. He and I need to talk now."

"Oh, right," Gabriel said. "Talk tomorrow?" he asked Gideon.

At Gideon's nod, he left his brother and father alone in the room.

The two men stared at each other, not speaking.

"Father?" Gideon finally said to test the waters. He needed to know if he was talking to the king or his father.

His father leaned forwarded and placed his hand on Gideon's shoulder. "You have done well in exposing Segenam. I had no idea of the evil that was lurking on this island. Thanks for allowing me to hold my head up again as a father."

Gideon felt his eyes tear and took a deep breath so as not to break down in front of his father.

"Shall I resume my regular duties, sir?" Gideon asked.

"Yes," the king replied. "Take a couple of days to catch up with the family and then get back to work. I definitely need your assistance."

"Who's been doing my work in the meantime?"

"My chief of staff offered to help me find an extra person to fill in, but I wasn't comfortable having too much information outside of the family," the king responded.

"That means there's a lot of work to be done," Gideon said, trying to suppress a sigh.

"You understand," his father said.

"Oh," Gideon said. "I almost forgot. Brother Adam is here from the temple. I'm assuming it is safe for him to return?"

The king responded, "It's safe at the temple, but he can stay for a while if you want him to act as your spiritual advisor."

"I don't need a spirit—" Gideon began but then stopped. "I'll consider it."

11

EDEN, FRIENDLY FIRE

"Ugh!" I said under my breath as I looked through my bag. I had forgotten my quilting project. After two years of sitting in Mrs. Askew's class, I knew enough to bring something to pass the time. Since I was sick of the dreary colors in my room, I had decided to make a quilt for my bed with brightly colored pieces of fabrics. There was a bin in the back of the classroom filled with leftover pieces of fabrics, but no one used it much. I had my choice of vibrant colors and patterns—turquoise, emerald, scarlet, striped, checked, polka dot, and so on.

Today, though, instead of rushing through the assignment so I could do my own project, I spent the two hours making barrettes. I resisted the urge to roll my eyes as Mrs. Askew chattered on about the joys of making one's own hair accessories.

I made a bunch of barrettes in blue and green colors. I noticed some of the other third-years preferred reds and pinks. I had avoided wearing red barrettes ever since I got spanked for stealing Lucinda's red barrette when I was six years old.

I cringed inwardly as I remembered well the scene. The pastor's voice was droning on and on, and I had fallen asleep, leaning on my mom's arm. When I woke up, the pastor was still going on, but my eyes were immediately drawn to a barrette with a bright red bow. It lay on the pew between me and Lucinda, who was a year or so older than me. The barrette belonged to her, but she was busy exchanging notes with her cousin sitting on the other side of her.

I still remembered the zing of happiness I felt as I picked up the barrette and held it in my hand. But Lucinda noticed right away that I took the barrette. She tried to pull it back from me, but I held on tighter. I just wanted to look at it. So, Lucinda and I commenced a tug-of-war over the barrette, which ended with our respective mothers grabbing us by the arms and half dragging and half pulling us out of the sanctuary and into the church dining hall.

Knowing I was in big trouble, I lied. I said Lucinda had given me the barrette to play with. A red-faced Lucinda countered that I was telling "a big fat lie." Of course, in the end, I had to give the lovely barrette back to Lucinda.

But the worst part yet was that in full view of Lucinda and her mother, my mother smacked my bottom hard and told me in a rough and gravelly voice that I would get worse if I ever lied again. My backside hurt, but I was more stunned by this new voice coming from my mother. From that moment on, if I heard her voice move anywhere close to rough and gravelly, I knew to tell the whole truth.

"You're crushing the barrette," I heard a voice say. Looking up, I saw it belonged to Annalise.

"Oh," I said as I opened my hand. The small rectangle metal piece had bent from the force of my clenched fist, and the blue velvet bow was half on and half off the metal.

I tried to bend the metal back to the correct shape and glued the fabric on again. After my repairs, the barrette still looked half-done. I would get maybe one good wear out of it. I decided not to include it in my final pile.

As Mrs. Askew made her rounds, checking on our progress, I noticed that only Jaelle, Bethany, and I had not used reds or pinks. While Kaitlyn had used a profusion of red, pink, and white lace, Jaelle had made her barrettes with costume pearls, and Bethany had made hers with black silk.

"What's the significance of the color red?" Mrs. Askew asked. "Annalise?"

"Meaning depends on context and culture," Annalise answered. The question had been on our final exam last year.

"Good answer," Mrs. Askew said. "Whenever you leave here, you must remember to make sure you follow the culture of your new home. Your new husbands should be able to help you not misstep."

Now, I really did roll my eyes. I thought I was subtle, but Mrs. Askew stopped at my table.

"Eden, I see you did your barrettes in greens and blues. Why didn't you pick red?" she asked.

"Red is the color of happiness," I responded, my face flushing as I realized the implications of that statement. I felt a bead of sweat trickle down the side of my face. "I meant that I associate red with happiness, but I like the serenity of blues and greens." Those Art of Conversation classes had some use after all.

"Thank you, Eden," Mrs. Askew said as she fanned at her face with hands. It was hot in the class. Most of the girls had taken their sweaters off. "Anyone else?"

"Yes, Jaelle," Mrs. Askew said in response to Jaelle's raised hand.

"Red is also the color of fire," she said, pointing to one of the room's two windows. We could see small flames flickering at the bottom of the window.

"Don't panic!" Mrs. Askew shouted above our expressions of dismay as she ran around to grab the fire extinguisher off the wall. "Everyone should walk calmly to the main exit," she said.

I was closest to the classroom door and reached it first, quickly grabbing the metal doorknob. Heat seared across my palm, and I yelled in pain. I moved back, holding my scalded hand as tears pricked my eyelids.

I heard a chorus of, "What are you doing?" "Move away!" and "We've got to get out of here!" The girls were crowding me.

In a panic, I screamed, "There's fire on the other side of the door!" I held up my reddened hand for everyone to see.

"Is there an emergency ladder?" Jaelle asked over the din of scared girls' crying.

"Is there an emergency ladder?" Mrs. Askew repeated, grabbing her head. "Yes! It's at the top of the closet, folded up. But I can't reach it!"

Jaelle was able to stand on a stool to reach the top of the closet. "I don't see it!" she shouted.

"Maybe we should just jump," Kaitlyn said, beads of sweat on her forehead.

"Where's the ladder?" Bethany's shrill voice yelled at Mrs. Askew.

"It's behind the box!" Mrs. Askew shouted.

An avalanche of old art supplies came raining down as Jaelle yanked the box from the top shelf.

"I got it!" she yelled, only her tiptoes remaining on the chair.

With my uninjured hand, I grabbed one of her calves to steady her, and someone else grabbed the other as she slid the ladder toward her. She needed both hands to hold the ladder as she jogged it over to the window without visible flames.

Mrs. Askew opened the window a small amount and peaked out. Smoke slipped through the opening. Several girls, including me, started to cough.

"It's smoke, but the fire is at the other window," Mrs. Askew said. Then she opened the window up all the way, and smoke billowed in.

As Mrs. Askew and Jaelle hooked the ladder on the window, the other girls and I tried to shield our noses and mouths as best we could with our shirts or any other piece of cloth we could find. Straining to remember fire safety tips from my childhood, I wondered if we should wet the material over our faces. But no water would come out of the faucets.

"The faucets aren't working!" I said, turning them on and off in disbelief.

"Let's go!" Bethany said, pulling me away.

"Move quickly, girls," Mrs. Askew ordered, and we did, for the most part, landing on damp ground. The gutter at the top of the building had been repaired a couple of days before, after leaking water down the back of the building and into squishy mud. The heat was rapidly drying the ground, so it was just a little damp.

After each girl came down the ladder, she ran off to a group of other Jade Vine House girls standing a good distance away. When I came down, I forced myself to ignore the flames all around the other window. After I hit the ground, I ran off and joined the girls from my house. Bethany, Annalise, and Jaelle were already there.

When I turned to look back at the burning building, I saw that Kaitlyn was cut off from joining us by two girls with masks holding sticks of fire in their hands. I don't know how they did it, but the fire remained at one end and didn't travel closer to their hands.

"Those girls are from one of the other houses," Annalise whispered, wheezing.

"Run, Kaitlyn!" I said, but I was doubled over and trying to breathe, causing my voice to come out a whisper-wheeze like Annalise's.

I stared at the scene in front of me, my home for the last two years engulfed in flames, the other girls crying and retching or dry heaving. Girls from the other houses stood a few feet away from my group. I was unnerved by their looks of grim satisfaction, their ugly smiles.

Some of them chanted, "Get her! Get her! Get her!" as the two girls with the fire sticks danced manically around Kaitlyn, their face masks making them look inhuman and sinister. Kaitlyn swayed from side to side, her face red and wet with a sheen of sweat. I looked all around, but there was no one to help: no fireman, no Mrs. Flint, and no teachers. Where was Mrs. Askew? I pushed that thought to the back of my mind as I saw Kaitlyn finally fall. One of the fire stick girls moved her fire closer toward Kaitlyn's back.

"No!" I screamed, and the girls with the fire sticks paused as heads turned in my direction. I took a wobbly step forward as my vision began to blur on the edges. I was out of air.

"Eden!" I heard Mr. Holt's voice say. "Get ahold of yourself!"

What is he doing here? I thought to myself as I met the ground rushing up to meet me.

WHEN I CAME TO, I was in the back seat of a car Mr. Holt was driving. There was a car in front and another car in back. Someone had put a raincoat on me.

"What's . . ." I started to say but then paused as a wave of nausea swept through me.

"Barf bag's in the seat pocket in front of you," Mr. Holt said, turning quickly around a curve along with the rest of the cars. I vomited into the bags, feeling dirty as I tasted the leftovers in my mouth. I tried to spit it all out, but I could still taste the residue.

"What happened?" I asked.

"Some girls from the other houses decided to set fire to the Jade Vine House. They had accelerants, which is why the house went up in flames so quickly."

"But what about the sprinklers?" I asked, certain I had seen some in the ceilings.

"Dismantled," Mr. Holt replied before hitting the steering wheel. "Damn it!" he yelled.

We had hit a traffic jam, and the cars were inching forward one miniscule inch at a time. Looking around, I could see nothing that was familiar. I was shocked at the sight of so many people.

"Where are we?" I asked, my head starting to throb. "Wait," I said. "Bethany? Kaitlyn? What happened to everyone?"

"Don't know," Mr. Holt replied. "My job was to extract you."

"But my friends!" I shouted, my voice sounded abnormally loud to me.

"I have someone checking on them," Mr. Holt replied tiredly as he looked around, trying to find some way to escape the traffic.

Feeling another wave of nausea and increased throbbing in my head, I closed my eyes and tried to breathe slowly, but my breath still felt shallow.

"How are you doing back there?" Mr. Holt replied, looking worried.

"I can't seem to catch my breath," I replied truthfully.

"We will get you treated as you soon as we get to the clinic," Mr. Holt replied. "Another twenty minutes."

"Umm," I replied as I looked out the window, noting the unfamiliarity again. "You never said. Where are we?"

"A safe place," he replied evasively.

"And that is?" I replied, annoyed.

"Untouchable City," Mr. Holt replied.

"But that's the city for sinners," I gasped.

"I got news for you, girl," Mr. Holt replied with a grim smile. "No city is without sinners. Didn't they teach you that in Sunday school?"

I suddenly felt very unsafe and shrank back into my seat.

Mr. Holt and the other two cars got off of the road and traveled down a street with lighter traffic. My eyes went wide at the people I saw. One woman wore a tight red shirt with no sleeves and no midriff, with a long orange flowing skirt adorned with a silvery belt. Her hair was short and dyed a shocking neon-green color. Another woman was dressed in a gray business suit with pants! Some of the men wore business suits, but some were dressed differently than I had ever seen, with long, twisted hair, markings on their face, and tight clothing accented with a lot of silver and leather. Some bopped their heads to music I couldn't hear.

"A little different than Sunny City," I heard Mr. Holt say.

I could only nod; I was so stunned.

"Don't worry," he said. "We'll get you treated, and then you'll be on your way to your fiancé."

"Who is he?" I asked, eager for any information.

"Hold on a sec," Mr. Holt replied as the car screen beeped, noting an incoming message.

I groaned in frustration.

"We're ready," a voice said.

"Good," Mr. Holt replied. "Eden, in thirty seconds, we are going to exit the car and leave the doors open. The decoys will take our place and drive to another hospital."

After a moment's hesitation, I nodded. I had to just trust Mr. Holt for now.

One minute later, I found myself inside the biggest hospital I had ever seen, with people moving purposely all around me.

"Hurry," Mr. Holt said. "This way."

We walked down a short hallway until we reached a door that stated, "Urgent Care Clinic." As soon as we walked in, a nurse led us through the waiting room, which was full of patients. My eye was caught by the one child in the room. He had eyes slanted slightly upward, and he smiled at me. But there was something about him that puzzled me.

Once in the examination room, the nurse checked my vitals while Mr. Holt paced and looked at his watch phone. Finally, the nurse was finished and told us the doctor would be in shortly.

As soon as she left, I asked Mr. Holt, "Did you see that toddler out there?"

"The one with Down Syndrome?" he replied.

I stared at him, shocked. "Isn't that illegal?"

Mr. Holt stopped pacing and said, "Look, Eden, everything is different in Untouchable City. People get knocked up all sorts of ways out here. They don't always follow the appropriate 'protocols.'" Mr. Holt used his fingers to demonstrate the quotations around the word "protocols."

"But . . ." I replied, my brain too befuddled to finish the question.

"But what?" Mr. Holt replied. "He shouldn't be alive?" He resumed pacing. "You need to get over your prejudice. You will see a lot of 'different' in this city. A lot of parents come to this city to give their children who are a little different a place to live."

"They can't live in their hometowns?" I asked and then answered my own question. "It would be presumed that they didn't follow the appropriate protocols?"

Mr. Holt nodded. "Then they would be found criminally negligent."

"And their babies taken from them?" I asked.

Mr. Holt agreed as the door opened. A middle-aged brown-skinned woman came in. She wore a physician's white coat. Women were even doctors in this city! I was starting to suspect there was a lot about this city I didn't know.

"Hi, Eden, I'm Dr. Brown," she said, smiling warmly as she held out her hand for me to shake.

"Nice to meet you," I replied automatically.

"Let's see. It says here you inhaled smoke due to a fire?" She looked at Mr. Holt instead of me.

"Don't ask," Mr. Holt replied.

"Got it," she answered curtly and pulled a curtain so she could examine me without Mr. Holt looking on.

After she finished, she pulled the curtain back and said to Mr. Holt, "I really would like to run some tests and look at an X-ray of her chest."

"No time," Mr. Holt replied. "We have to get out of here. Can she make it another forty-eight hours?"

"She can," the doctor replied. "But she should be seen and treated as soon as she arrives. I'm going to give her a bronchodilator and a steroid so she can breathe easier."

"Give her something to help if she gets nervous flying too," Mr. Holt said.

"How old are you?" she asked me. "Some medications I can't give you if you're under the age of consent."

"I'm sixteen," I replied.

"Date of birth?" she asked, looking at her electronic notepad.

"October 14, 2121," I replied.

She didn't respond, just tilted her head as though trying to remember something. I noticed her hands start to shake before she turned away from me, her back ramrod straight.

"Is there something I should know?" Dr. Brown asked.

"Not now," Mr. Holt said firmly. "Give her the medicine. We've already been here too long."

"Please," she said, her voice begging.

Uncomfortable, I looked to Mr. Holt. His face was impassive, giving nothing away.

"For her safety, I need you to just be her doctor," he said, unyielding.

She wilted and shuffled to the door, the confident doctor gone and, in her place, a defeated woman.

Mr. Holt exhaled slowly and walked around the room as we waited for her return. I wondered about his exchange with the doctor, but with the tiredness in my body, the thoughts were fleeting. As soon as my eyelids fluttered closed, the door opened again, and I sighed.

The doctor jammed the medications into Mr. Holt's hand, her pressed lips indicating her displeasure. She then released a breath and turned to me with a tremulous smile. "I hope to see you again, Eden," she said. "I will be praying for your safety." She then stepped forward and hugged me hard. I wondered if doctors were supposed to hug their patients.

"Ouch!" I said as I felt a hair get caught on something.

When I wiggled out of her embrace, I saw that she held a few of my hairs in her hand.

"Sorry," she said. "They must have gotten caught on my button."

"Dr. Brown," Mr. Holt began in a warning tone.

"Don't you have to go?" the doctor replied, a hint of challenge in her eyes.

"I'm ready," I said to Mr. Holt as I jumped off the table. I swayed a little bit but then steadied.

Mr. Holt hesitated, but then he handed me a bag and said, "You've got three minutes." Inside the bag were a bouncy, curly blonde wig, jeans, and a t-shirt. The wig reminded me of Kaitlyn and my other friends.

"God, please let them all be alive!" I prayed as I dressed.

Despite myself, when we arrived at Untouchable City's airport, I felt a small frisson of excitement at the idea of flying in an airplane. The airport was huge, and there were tons of people moving in a hurry. But Mr. Holt drove me to a section that was quite quiet, for private flights only.

"I can't go with you," Mr. Holt said as he handed me my medication and a passport. "Remember that a Mr. Holmes should meet you when you land at Heathrow, and then you will fly to Seahorse Island."

Mr. Holt boarded the plane with me and then spoke to the pilot and a flight attendant. Before he deplaned, he looked me up and down, his brows scrunched together in concern. "You all right?"

"You haven't told me about my fiancé," I said.

"You'll meet him soon. Remember to give him the greeting I taught you, the one you use for social superiors."

12

GIDEON, LINE OF SUCCESSION

Six weeks after his return to the palace, Gideon stood in the nursery, staring at his niece, Amara, as she stared solemnly back at him. She was so very tiny and light in his two hands that her fragility humbled him. He rarely got to interact with her. Her twin, Aditya, tended to be the more demanding of the two girls, so he had held her plenty in the past weeks. Amara either slept the blissful sleep of newborns or looked on quietly as Aditya cried and fussed. Now Aditya was with Lily and his mother, playing on the other side of the nursery, and Amara was awake. After continuing to stare at him for a moment, Amara finally smiled at him.

"I got it!" he whisper-shouted as he smiled back.

Amara promptly started crying at his enthusiasm, which set Aditya to crying as well.

"Nice going," his brother said with a smirk as he reached over to take his daughter.

She immediately settled down and looked at Gideon almost accusingly from the safe cocoon of her father's arms.

"I didn't hear you come in," Gideon said to Gabriel.

"I know, you and Amara were having a mutual admiration society meeting," Gabriel said.

"Babies need quiet, Gideon," Lily said as she stood and rocked Aditya.

"No, they don't," Gideon's mother said. "Babies need to get used to noise. That's the problem with children nowadays. Too much coddling."

Lily looked stricken for a moment, and she forgot to continue to rock Aditya, until the baby cried even louder in indignation.

"Nonsense," Ya Ya said from the doorway. "Babies can never be coddled too much." She walked over and cooed and smiled at Aditya, her dark eyes alive and bright.

Aditya stopped fussing and grabbed her great-grandmother's finger.

Ya Ya turned back to her daughter-in-law with her hands on her hip. "Didn't you fire your twins' nanny for forgetting to put her phone on vibrate while they were sleeping?"

"Their father talked me out of that, Mother, as you well know," the queen said before she walked out of the nursery with slightly less than her usual grace.

Lily visibly relaxed, and Gideon decided it would be a good time to exit as well. As much as he loved his nieces, he was quite ready for lunch, and he had a tight afternoon schedule.

"Ah, Gideon." Ya Ya interrupted his leave-taking. "Have you seen Adam?"

"I haven't seen him all morning," Gideon replied as he tried to walk around her. "I'll tell him you want to talk with him if I see him."

His grandmother put out a hand to stop him. "Why are you avoiding him?"

Gideon sighed while leaning his back against the doorframe and putting his hands in his pockets. "Ya Ya, I'm not avoiding him. I have a lot of work to do, and I'm still catching up from the time I spent away."

"Um, is that so?" His grandmother looked at him skeptically before one of the twins cried again and diverted her attention.

As Gideon walked away quickly, he frowned. He loved being part of his family. It soothed something within him to know he was still loved by everyone who was important to him. They welcomed him back with open arms and no words of recrimination. And yet, there was a part of him that felt he didn't deserve their forgiveness and love. By indulging in his most improper desires, he had almost brought about the death of his brother. He had certainly killed any chance his brother had of fathering more children. Amara and Aditya had been born using embryos that Lily and Gabriel had frozen. There weren't any more spare embryos, and the doctors had confirmed Gabriel's unviable sperm.

Thoughts of these things had become like a twisted wreath of heavy, jagged stones around his neck. At times, his steps faltered, and he staggered from the weight and pinch of stones visible only to the eyes of the guilty. There was only so much he could unburden to his twin, and he hadn't made time to speak with Brother Adam in all the weeks he had been back. He dealt with his feelings by keeping busy, swimming laps before his work day, and then working until late at night or the very early morning hours. If he took time to eat away from his desk, he ate with someone from his family, and he usually peeked in on his nieces daily. He intended to make good his resolve to be a better brother, uncle, grandson, and son. He didn't have time to waste by talking about his inner life with the too-perceptive Brother Adam.

On his arrival back at his office, Gideon's stomach growled, but he didn't see his lunch waiting on his desk as he ordered. His assistant wasn't sitting at his desk right outside Gideon's office, either. Gideon felt himself get irritated at the thought that his assistant had gone to lunch and forgot to order lunch for Gideon. He would have to order his own lunch.

"Sir." Gideon's assistant hurried into his office. "I was just in the washroom. Your mother requested your presence in the family dining room for lunch."

"But I have a meeting in twenty minutes," Gideon said, further irritated.

"It was rescheduled," his assistant said.

"You rescheduled a meeting because my mother requested lunch?" Gideon asked, incredulous.

"Sir, the person you were supposed to meet with, Prince Jordain, had to reschedule due to a family emergency," the assistant answered. "He sent his apologies. Also, your mother said your father would be at the lunch as well."

"I see," Gideon said in a questioning tone. His family tried to eat together for dinner, but lunch was more ad hoc. It was certainly rare for both his father and mother to request his presence for lunch. Maybe they wanted to talk about the marriage. His body filled with dread.

"Did she indicate anything else?" Gideon asked carefully.

"No, sir," the assistant replied guilelessly.

Gideon took a deep breath, heard his stomach growl again in demand for food, and walked toward the Li Family dining room in the royal family's private area. Only family members ate in this dining room, no guests. For some reason, the architect had designed the room so that it was round. It had been decorated with lavender and silver accents and, per the queen's mandate, filled with an array of fragrant island flowers. The round table was topped with deep-purple granite.

It was Gideon's favorite room in which to dine. He and Gabe had been forced to eat in the nursery until they were thirteen. No amount of begging or pleading would get his parents to relent prior to that time. Gideon would never admit how very pleased he had been when he and Gabe had finally been admitted to the "adult" dining room. As he walked toward it, his mouth watered from the enticing aroma of thoroughly spiced food, even as his stomach twisted as he guessed the reason for his mother's summons.

"Gideon, you came." His mother greeted him with a hug, momentarily ensconcing him with warm arms and the citrus-spiced scent she wore. His mother hugged him a lot these days.

"Of course," he said, pulling back to smile at her. His mother could be noisy and intrusive, but he knew she loved him.

"We'll eat a la carte today, but I had the chef make your favorites, sesame ginger chicken and pot stickers. Also, for dessert—"

"Jasmine, are you a waitress?" King Edward queried his wife. "Let the boy get his food so we can eat." The king had a bowl of ox bone soup in front of him.

Gideon had swallowed one delicious bite of sesame ginger chicken, when his mother started the conversation. "The line of succession depends on you," she stated baldly.

Gideon's father sighed and said, "Jasmine, must we do this now? Can't it wait until at least the coffee is served?"

Gideon nearly choked on his water. "What are you talking about?"

Queen Jasmine looked at him as though he were a simpleton. "Lily had girls."

Gideon looked at her before daring to speak what had been on his mind for some time. "Can't father issue some sort of decree so girls can inherit?"

"It's in the Royal Rules of State enacted during the early days of the island. It's one of the few rules I can't change," the king said. "At least, not without a vote from all the communal leaders agreeing."

"You don't think they will?" Gideon asked, surprised. "Have we asked for a change to the Royal Rules before?"

"No," his father answered. "And I don't intend to start now. With all the upheaval caused by Sector 16, everyone is trying to take advantage of the shifting power balance."

"I'm so sorry. It's my fault," his mother said, starting to cry.

Gideon stared at her, uncomprehending.

"No, Jasmine, the fault is all mine," his father replied.

"What are you talking about?" Gideon asked, impatience seeping into his voice.

"Son, we have a confession," his father replied, his face reddening. "When I saw your mother, I knew I wanted to marry her and no one else."

"Okay?" Gideon replied, still confused.

"But your mother wasn't the best genetic match," his father said.

His mother continued, "But we knew a doctor who could modify the gene that made me incompatible, and he confirmed it well enough that your father and I felt safe marrying."

"I know you got married," Gideon said. "Was there another kid or something?" he asked, shocked at the thought even as he asked the question.

"No, no," his mother said, her face very red. "When we went to the doctor to have the embryo that had been genetically modified implanted, the doctor discovered I was already a week or so pregnant with you."

"I have the defective gene?" Gideon asked.

At his parents' embarrassed nods, Gideon said, "Gabriel really is the perfect child, and I am the defective version." He stood up and threw his fork on the table, immediately regretting the rude action but unable to speak through the sudden tightness in his throat.

"Gideon—" his mother started to say, but Gideon ignored her and stalked out of the dining room and his family's personal quarters.

He intended to head back to his office, but he felt too bothered to sit at his desk. Looking at his watch phone, he saw he had time before his next meeting, so he decided to visit the east garden and walk the tension off.

As he opened the door to the garden, the wind flew in, making him shiver with cold. He needed a coat, so he held the door open with one hand and reached over to grab his coat off a nearby hook.

"Do you think Prince Gideon suspects?" Gideon heard a voice ask. He realized it was coming from the garden, but he didn't see anyone.

"I told you not to mention him by name," an irritated voice replied.

Gideon's eyes widened as he recognized the voice of his father's chief of staff.

"Sorry, sir," said a contrite voice, one that Gideon didn't recognize.

"I take it that the package has been redirected?" the chief of staff asked the unknown man.

"Yes, to The Glass House as you instructed," said the unknown man.

"Prince, do you need a warmer coat?" One of the palace staffers was hurrying over with a long down coat that was much warmer than the coat in his hand.

Gideon cursed inwardly. "No, it's all good. I was just about to take a walk." Just then, Gideon's watch phone pinged and then pinged multiple times in succession. It was his mom, Gabe, Luke, and James, all wondering where he was.

Sighing, Gideon let go of the door, put the coat back on the hook, and returned to the family dining room, dreading a continuation of the conversation he had deserted.

Once at the dining room's elegant double doors, Gideon took a deep breath and opened a door. Only his father was in the room.

"Where's mom?" he asked.

His father replied, "She went to see to something. She will be back in a few minutes."

As he sat down, Gideon wished his mother was present. The atmosphere was tense.

"Two whiskeys, sir." A server came in and put a whiskey in front of each man.

"Can you remove my whiskey and bring seltzer water and lime?" Gideon asked.

He was annoyed when he saw the server look to his father for permission before removing the whiskey, saying, "Of course, sir."

"You don't like the whiskey?" his father asked.

"I'm avoiding alcohol after . . . after everything," Gideon said, wishing his father would get to the point.

His father only nodded and took a sip of his own whiskey. His father's throat moved as he swallowed, and Gideon suddenly remembered how he loved the warmth that filled his body after a sip of whiskey. After his father's third sip, Gideon, in desperation, decided to go on the offensive.

"You want me to get married and have sons?" he asked. "I can't guarantee the sons, but I can get married. Do I get to choose her?"

His father took another sip of whiskey before replying, "I'm hoping you agree with our choice. She was chosen with you in mind."

That was a definitive no on getting to choose his own bride. "Whom do I marry?" Gideon willed his leg not to bounce up and down. He didn't want to get married, and he was unsettled by the urgency with which his parents were treating his marriage. He had promised himself that he would be a better son. He had not envisioned that part of being a better son was allowing his parents to pick his bride.

"You don't know her," his father replied.

"I think I know all the eligible women of suitable families," Gideon replied. Apart from Angel, he had made sure to keep his interest limited to women whose family background would never be acceptable for a royal marriage. At his father's look, which said he knew exactly what his son had been doing, Gideon shrugged.

"As I said, you don't know her. She's from America," his father said, barely keeping the distaste from his voice.

"America?" Gideon asked, astonished. America had been trying for greater influence on the island for years. "That country executed its own president because she refused to bow down to those militia groups." He shuddered as he remembered the images of all the executions and chaos that followed. Some streets in America had literally run red with blood. It was as if hell had been turned loose on earth.

"I know," his father said. "But the problem is, if you marry someone on the island, you will be required to share your gene map. The defective gene only activates if both the parents have the gene, so it probably wouldn't be a problem in actuality, since the gene is not common here. But the real problem is, the existence of the defective gene would be hard to keep secret in a marriage negotiation."

"Is that bad?" Gideon asked.

"It would be embarrassing," his father said. "The defective gene causes white pupils."

"Oh. Is that where the eyes look as though they have no color? The entire eye looks white?" Gideon asked.

"Yes, the person can still see, but it's hard for others to look at them," his father replied.

"It's very creepy," Queen Jasmine said from the doorway and delicately shivered. "Your father and I should have been more consistent in our use of birth control, but then you wouldn't be here if we had been."

"Thanks, I think," Gideon replied, standing upon his mother's entry into the dining room.

"Don't worry," his mother said as she sat down and motioned for him to do the same. "We found a nice girl for you to marry. She's from America, but she has no family to ask probing questions. Best of all, she's a great genetic match."

"Plus, your mother will have plenty of time to mold her," his father said.

"How old is she?" Gideon asked.

"Sixteen," his mother replied, holding up a hand to stop his next question. "You won't marry her until she's around twenty-three."

"That's seven years away," his father said.

"I can count," Gideon said sarcastically before taking a deep breath. "Sorry, Father, Mother, but this is all a little sudden. You've seen me date other girls without saying anything."

"We knew you weren't serious," his mother said, looking at him sympathetically. "The only one who gave us pause was Angel."

"And she turned out to be a demon from hell," his father said. "The girl we have chosen will be a much better fit for you."

"How do you know?" Gideon asked, genuinely puzzled.

"She has been trained to be a good wife to a high-ranking man," his mother replied.

"Wait, she doesn't go to the school we were discussing when I first got back, does she? The one mentioned by the minister of internal security?" Gideon didn't say more because he wasn't sure how much he could say in front of his mother.

"She attends the school you're thinking of," his father said before taking another sip of whiskey.

"Isn't that a bit hypocritical? Do those girls have any say? Or is she like a robot?" Gideon asked, nauseated. He mimicked a robot, straightening his back and moving his arms straight up and down while saying in an electronic voice, "Would you like dinner, sir?"

"Enough," his father commanded. "Act your age."

"That was immature," Gideon agreed. "But couldn't you have someone put together a dossier on a bunch of genetically compatible potentials?"

"Mother is the one who directed us to her," the king said.

"Mother?" Gideon asked, looking at his mother before realizing she was not who his father meant. "Oh, you mean Ya Ya? Don't tell me. She had a dream?"

Gideon had meant the question sarcastically, but his father answered in the affirmative. "She dreamed of a school full of brides, and she said the school was in America in the dream."

"That was the basis for your selection?" Gideon asked.

"We looked at a number of bios from the school, and she was the best genetic match. The girl seems nice enough. She's been raised well, but she really doesn't have any other good options."

Seeing the incredulous look on her son's face, Gideon's mother hurriedly interrupted. "She should be here soon, next day or so."

"What do you mean by 'here'?" Gideon asked. "At the palace?"

"Yes," Queen Jasmine said with a satisfied smile. "She will be our ward."

"Wait, don't tell me she's going to live here," Gideon said, aghast.

"Only for two years," Gideon's mother said. "Well, only for the two years that she will be educated at the palace. Then she will go to college for four years and study political science before becoming engaged to you. The wedding would be in May of the following year."

"See, your mother has everything all planned out," his father said. "Don't worry."

Gideon worried. "This plan is too convoluted. The worst that can happen if I marry someone from the island is that people will know I carry this gene. That's it; that's the worst. But if I marry an American, the sectors will practically revolt."

"Then you will have seven years to build up goodwill," the king said.

"It bothers you that much that people know that we carry the 'white pupil' gene?" Gideon asked.

"It happens more among poor individuals," his father explained.

"If they had money, they wouldn't have continued the gene." His mother shrugged one shoulder.

Gideon shook his head, refusing to believe his parents were that vain. "What happens if I refuse? I won't marry an islander, since you are so concerned about the defective gene, but I want to choose my own bride."

"I can't force you to marry her," his father said. "But as you well know, you can't marry without my consent."

"I will go along with things for now," Gideon replied. "But if we find we don't suit each other toward the end of seven years, you have to find someone else to marry her." Gideon held his breath as he waited for his father's response.

"Fair enough," his father said. Gideon felt as though he had won a huge victory.

"Just out of curiosity," Gideon said, "what is the line of succession? It's Gabe, then me, and then—not Amara or Aditya. But then the next male heirs would be Simon and his sons?"

"Your cousin Simon has more illegitimate than legitimate sons," his father said. "The fighting over the crown would throw the island into chaos."

Before his mother could respond, one of his father's staffers appeared at the door and waited to be acknowledged. His father waved her over.

"Sir, the contact to pick up the ward says she never showed."

His father stood up, his face a mask of displeasure. "What do you mean?"

The staffer replied, "She never met Mr. Holmes at the Heathrow Airport, sir. We have all available personnel tracking cameras and video feed."

Queen Jasmine gasped as she grasped the implications.

The king stood and looked at Gideon and the queen. "Excuse me. We'll need to continue this conversation later."

Gideon thought about the earlier conversation he had overheard. "If I may have a minute, Father."

"Yes," the king responded, clearly impatient.

Gideon looked at the staffer, whose lips tightened as she understood that Gideon wanted her to leave. She quickly bowed at her waist and exited.

"Gideon, what is it? I have to go handle this situation," his father said, walking toward the door and indicating that Gideon should walk with him.

"Could she be at The Glass House?" Gideon asked.

At his father's surprised look, Gideon hurried to say, "I overhead your chief of staff talking with someone, saying the package had been redirected to The Glass House."

The two men looked at each other as they stood at the door. "He wouldn't," Gideon's father said.

"I'm not sure," Gideon responded. "With all the changes for Sector 16, maybe he feels she gives him some sort of leverage?"

The king's face hardened. "Let's see what is being delivered to The Glass House. If it's the girl, I need her extracted and brought here."

"I can handle it," Gideon said.

His father stared at him before saying, "Yes, I think you can. Do you need assistance from the U.K.?"

"I planned to use the captain and his special operations team, but it would be helpful to have U.K.'s assistance," Gideon replied. "The Glass House is in their country."

"I'll arrange it quietly," his father said.

"I'll need a picture and details on her arrangements," Gideon said. "Can you have that information sent electronically?"

"Consider it done," his father replied.

Gideon nodded to both his parents, gathered up James and Luke and three other royal guard members, and was in the air in half an hour. The supersonic jet was kept ready for emergencies. The captain and his team would meet up with them in the U.K.

A few minutes later, he opened his notepad and stared at the image that appeared. It was the knitting girl, the girl from his dreams. This time she looked directly at him.

13

EDEN, RESCUE ME

*L*ess than seven hours later after I left Mr. Holt, I was being driven on a narrow road hemmed in on both sides by tall, overarching trees illuminated by white headlights that made them look almost sinister against the palpable darkness. The blackened trunks of the trees were thick with age, but every once and a while, the headlights showed the slender bending rail of a new tree that had taken root.

There were two cars in front and two cars behind me, so we were a small caravan. Mr. Holmes indicated that we would stay overnight at something called The Glass House and then fly out to Seahorse Island in a day or two.

The wind blew around us with light gusts so that crinkly autumn leaves rustled past the sleek cars, sounding abnormally loud on the quiet road. Still, no matter the gentle rustling, I imagined the wind as just temporarily restrained, like a child taking a breather before the next tantrum. The wind even smelled different, carrying scents still strange to me.

I was in a foreign country before I traveled to another foreign country to meet my fiancé, a man with whom I had never met or spoken. I was in no great rush to meet him. I was marrying him because I had no other options. Why he wanted to marry me, I had no idea.

A mere two days ago, I thought I had time to figure it all out, but now I found myself traveling on a road far from any home I had ever known. I missed my friends: Kaitlyn, Bethany, Annalise, and Jaelle. I prayed for their safety and hoped Mr. Holt would get word to me about them soon. I wondered if the girls who set the fire that night were in prison.

I shook my head and tried to calm myself. Relief, however, remained elusive. The thick darkness of night pressed heavily against the sleek, dark car, and the adrenaline that had accompanied me thus far rapidly dissipated.

My hands trembled slightly, and I clasped them together. I hadn't had a restful sleep in a while, so my right eye was furiously ticking as it was wont to do when I was tired. My stomach muscles clenched almost painfully, feeding more off nerves than food. More disturbing was the mushrooming headache that threatened my resolve to avoid crying.

I was on the verge of asking the driver to stop so I could step out of the car and attempt to take a breath that wasn't too shallow or panicky, but then the heavy press of trees began to noticeably thin. The driver started a tuneless whistle. A short time later, we finally left the trees altogether, and I gasped in surprise.

It was as if in an instant I left Hades's dark forest and floated into a more beautiful world. A full moon hung swollen and round, dressed in gauzy clouds drifting dreamily against an immense sheet of night sky adorned with sparkling stars. If only I could crawl out of the car and lie down to rest under such a beautiful sky!

I had expected the moon to keep watch over an old English mansion, the kind described in the books I was allowed to read at school. While the house was certainly massive in size, it was entirely modern in design, about three levels with the side facing the car made entirely of clear glass, except for a pair of side-by-side doors which were opaque. The roof was jagged and uneven by design. Despite its size, the house gave the impression of having grown out of the ground.

Forgetting I was supposed to wait for the driver, I opened the car door, intending to step out of Hades and into a brand-new life. Hopefully, a better life and not just a new level of hell.

As soon as I fully stepped out, I heard a rustling, and then a shadow moved straight at me.

What now? I panicked as it grabbed me by the waist and literally threw me. A weight pressed on my back, and a hand covered my mouth.

I remembered ice-blue eyes from my first kidnapping and resolved to fight. I struggled, but it was the same as the first time. I couldn't get any leverage.

Tears ran down my face, and I jerked as I heard loud booms, one right after the other. Were they gunshots? The fear that spiked through my already-compromised body had me on the verge of fainting, but I couldn't give up struggling, even though I knew I was weakening.

The weight on me suddenly lifted, and I greedily sucked in air.

As I braced my hands on the ground in preparation for getting up, I noticed shifting beneath the dirt. An adder snake, thick with ebony scales, raised its head and hissed at me.

As I lay there, frozen, a muscular bronzed arm reached out and grabbed the snake by its tail. After the snake disappeared from my view, I came to my senses, remembering the danger I was in.

I turned to see who was behind me and looked up at a tall man. Blood had spattered on his black combat boots and fatigues. There was no question he was the victor of whatever fight had just happened. He gripped a long rifle in his left hand, with no sign of injury. Every inch of him screamed fighter. His eyes, however, were filled with compassion and warmth. He looked at me as though he knew me.

He reached out his hand and said, "My bride, I presume?"

AFTERWORD

Thank you for reading *BECOMING PRINCESS EDEN—Book One: How They Met*! I hope you enjoyed the beginning of Eden and Gideon's story.

If you want to get updates about new releases visit my website: https://www.LisaLeeWrites.com. I love to hear from readers, so please feel free to leave a comment!

If you enjoyed this story, please leave a review and tell your friends.

ACKNOWLEDGMENTS

Thank you to the Almighty and everyone who made this book possible:
My husband, David, for encouraging me to keep writing.
My kids, Faith and Solomon, for being patient with me when I am in
writing mode. I love you both—equally!

To the University of Chicago Graham School Writer's Studio, for
helping improve my writing.

To Christina Schrunk, for being the world's most amazing editor!

To Maria Castro, Dr. Elizabeth Drame, Lydia Hall, Shawna Paterson,
Christine Powell, Jendayi Ricardo, and Deborah Williams, for
encouragement, prayer, and feedback. A special thank you to Kim
Gibson who encouraged me from the very beginning.

To Clean Indie Reads (C.I.R) writers, for sharing so much knowledge!

www.ingramcontent.com/pod-product-compliance
Lightning Source LLC
Chambersburg PA
CBHW022106170626
46808CB00002B/627